Orion's Honor

Melissa Koons

Orion's Honor
2nd Edition
Revised and edited for some language and content
Copyright 2018 Write Illusion LLC
ISBN Paperback: 978-1-7324422-1-4
ISBN eBook: 978-1-7324422-0-7
Previously released as "John: A Tale of a Knight"
Winner of the Editor's Choice Award at iUniverse 2013
Cover art designed by Sebastian Hernandez and Melissa Koons
Formatting designed by Write Illusion LLC

W

www.writeillusionllc.com

For my family and friends who always support me

Melissa Koons

Prologue

Every hero has a story; this is an inarguable fact, because without the story, there is no hero. Without the story, there is just a man that did something heroic that no one saw. Without the story, there is no heroism, just an action. Some heroes' stories aren't much. Some stories are dull and long; others are exciting but short. Whatever type of story it is, whether it is an epic or a short, exciting or excitingly boring, it is the story that proves the hero. The story is the evidence of a heroic act. The question, then, is, what makes the hero? Some heroes were gallant men with a strange sense of nobility that went searching for adventure and damsels to rescue. Some heroes were just men in the right place at the right time with the balls to do something about it. But is that all a hero is? Is the hero just the guy that has the balls to do something about it?

I was not the charge-into-action type. I wasn't born with a sense of nobility or do-gooder heroism (much to my mother's disappointment.) I was more of the sit-back-and-talk-someone-else-into-it type. My best friend, though, he was born with a strange sense of nobility and honor. He was born with valor and the desire to actively seek trouble just so he could solve it. Ever since we were boys, John always wanted to be a hero; he wanted to be the knight in shining armor who saved the day. Ever since his mother began reading to him the tales of King Arthur and the knights of his round table, John couldn't get it out of his head.

John and I grew up together, nearly brothers, but blessed with the closeness of nonrelation. John and I were complete opposites of each other. He had light-blond hair that was always nicely trimmed and blue eyes he had gotten from his mother; I, on the other hand, had almost-black shaggy hair and dark-brown eyes. John was always patient and far tamer than my mother ever dreamed I could be. I was much rasher and couldn't keep my mouth shut to save my life. John was more of the quiet type that took his time to think things through before he acted. It's a good thing we had each other; we balanced each other out.

We met—god, I can't even recall; it's been that long. You know when someone important comes into your life and when you think back to that moment, or even that day that you met, you draw a complete blank because all you know, and all you need to know, is that they changed your life for the better? I say "for the better" because when bad people enter our lives, we always seem to remember the exact day down to the very detail of what we ate for breakfast the morning before. See, I remember the day I met that crook Jake and he robbed me of my lunch in grade school; I remember the day that I met Susan, the prostitute who worked on Twelfth Street; and I remember the day I met our recruiter, Col. Howard Lee Brice. Coincidentally, I think I had eggs for breakfast on all of these days— but I don't remember when I met John.

John was just there. Regardless, he became my best friend, and since that day in our youth that we met, we did everything together; we were all each other had and all each other needed. My mother always set a spot for John at dinner, and occasionally lunch. Pretty soon John was there for every meal; he nearly became a live-in.

John's mom was beautiful; she was the first woman I ever fell in love with, and the first woman I ever masturbated to. Mrs. Cummings loved John; he was her world. It only took one look into that creamy face, with those blue eyes, those red lips, all framed by her sunny-yellow hair, to know that he was her life and her whole world. She did whatever she had to for him; perhaps that was her reasoning for staying with that man, although it seemed like a leap out of the frying pan and straight into the fire more than a solution.

When we played, John always used to pretend that he was Sir Lancelot from the gallant tales of King Arthur and his court. "Come on, Ben! It'll be fun!" John urged me along.

I remember, even then, being in awe of the energy that he had. John always had this particular energy that could never be exhausted. It wasn't just the typical energy of a boy that only wanted to run and play; no, John had his own kind of energy. John's energy was a kind of essence that came from deep within him and spread outward. He didn't need the help of sugar or other stimulants to give him a boost. He didn't even have to smile, which was a rare occurrence indeed after he turned twelve. John's energy was more than just movement; it was something warm and inviting that pulled everyone around him into it and made them feel just what he felt. John could do that; he just naturally had it.

John and I had many exploits together. We got into trouble at every turn. After all, it was a small town and Sheriff Hanson lived two doors down from me. It also probably didn't help that my pop was the deputy. Perhaps that was why we got caught so much—that and our being the only boys in the town that had the balls to do what we did. Oh, it was nothing exactly criminal—although we did spend a good many Friday nights in the jail cells at the sheriff's office— just a few scarecrow rearranging here and there when we were younger, then some joyriding in my father's truck, some charges of disorderly conduct for leaving the bar particularly noisily, and I think we might have stolen some chickens from Mr. Walsenburg once or twice (we gave them back, of course.) I think it was all of these "heinous crimes" that compelled my mother to allow us to enter the military. She cried when we left for boot camp, and she cried when our summons for the war came, but she never tried to stop us; I think she knew we were bigger than what our little town had to offer.

John was the one that got the pamphlets for the Marines. "It would be a great adventure" he said, and when those cornflower-blue eyes of his lit up in such excitement, I had no prayer to deny him. I could never deny him; he had too many people doing that already. I must admit I was astonished when he came home that day with his idea. I never expected John to be one for the military; I never expected I'd join him, either. Neither of us were particularly good at following orders. We liked to do things our own way, and the military did not like you to do anything unless it was their way.

A lot of folks were proud when we announced that we were joining—or, I should say, a lot of people were proud when John announced that he was joining; naturally, they expected me to follow, as I always did. Some people might be offended to say that people expected them to follow someone else, and if it had been anyone but John I might have been, but with John, how could I not? It was that energy of his. It just brought others in and wrapped around them so tight that they couldn't escape—and they never wanted to. As long as you could feel that warm energy of his, you wanted to follow him anywhere just to never be without it.

Everyone in Greenwood County was over-joyed by our declaration; Uncle Sam wanted us to join and the whole town was ready to spend what little money they had on war bonds to support us. They congratulated us, wide smiles plastered to their faces as they shook our hands and all the hands of the boys who enlisted from our town. I stood off to the side as people asked their silent questions of John, those thousands of eyes, two by two, forming their own accusations, their own stories—"It must have been that Dragon of his" and the like.

I wasn't so sure of his motivation to join; I wasn't sure that the rumors of his Dragon weren't the truth; I just knew that the pressure from the government and the propaganda posters and clips in the moving pictures were enough to shame me into it even if John hadn't suggested it first. When he showed me those pamphlets he got from Col. Howard Lee Brice at the recruitment office, he had this drained look to him like a half-drowned cat clinging to the life boat that would steer it away from the floods.

"We need something bigger; we're knights, after all," John said to me with a smile. It was a slight smile that turned up the corners of his lips and that was it. I nodded my agreement, and the spark immediately came back, although only half as bright. So while everyone congratulated us and celebrated our courage, I looked over at John and knew that he needed to feel the cold steel of a rifle in his hands before he felt those hands were worthy of belonging to a knight.

October 1941

The air was warm and heavy with moisture. Every morning I would wake up feeling a thin layer of moisture along my skin that never seemed to leave. Kansas was humid, but Wake Island was worse. The breeze would come off of the Pacific Ocean and bring with it tiny droplets of water. John and I had been stationed here since September, and even though it was approaching December, the temperature never seemed to show it. The days ran together, bright and sunny with a few rain clouds here and there but nothing to distinguish one hour from another.

The Marine Corps wasn't what I thought it would be, but then again, I really didn't have any expectations of what it would be like anyway. John was the one that picked the Marines by saying, "When it comes to being knightly, the Marines carry the sword." I was fine with that; at least we didn't have to dig trenches in Germany.

We were specifically stationed on Peale Island, the small atoll on the north side of Wake. For the first month we were stationed we didn't have a whole lot to do. It wasn't until Major Devereux arrived at the beginning of October that he began pushing us all to fortify this damned place. We ate, did drills, checked the equipment, constructed the airstrip, and reinforced the island's security. That was about it, but it was still plenty to do. I would lie in my cot for a few minutes, trying to remember the Kansas sun and the sound of birds other than those stupid rail birds that wandered the island. I'd gotten into the habit of waking up a few minutes before reveille because I liked the serenity. John slept in the cot beside mine, and he never seemed to pause and think about what it was we were doing there. I think that's because somewhere in his mind we weren't really on a tropical island in the Pacific Ocean, but off on some quest clad in shiny silver armor with swords instead of guns.

I waited for the horns to sound the wakeup call, listening to the troops on duty squish through the sand. That's all that fucking island was: sand. There were trees and lush tropical vegetation, but that was on the side of the island that John and I were not stationed at. All we had on our side of the island were tiny palms that would let the moist sun shine right through and pierce our flesh. I wasn't looking forward to the day's duties, and not for the first time, I wondered why I had let John convince me to sign up. Sure, he pulled that whole "we're knights in need of an adventure" spiel, but looking back I wonder if that's the real reason I agreed. The horns sounded, and I looked over to the bunk beside mine and watched as John's eyes slowly opened. He sat up and immediately began getting his uniform on while I simply sat up and picked up one of my boots, turning it upside down to let the sand pour out.

"Come on, Ben. I know it's never nice to be woken up by that horn, but you've got to get used to it."

I just nodded and ignored the urge to tell him that those horns had never woken me up. It wouldn't have done me any good if he knew I was already awake when the horns went off; he'd just scold me even more for not getting ready fast enough.

"I hope the mail arrives today; it's been a few weeks since we've heard anything from the mainland. I wonder how Mom's doing," John said as he tucked in his shirt. He mumbled some other things into his chest as he tightened his belt. I knew he really just wanted to hear about Red. Had she moved on? Was she waiting for him? I watched as his eyes unfocused and he drifted off, thinking of her—her white skin, the soft freckles that dotted the bridge of her nose, and those eyes. Ah, how he thought of those eyes. I'd caught him once or twice drawing those almond-shaped eyes of hers on scrap pieces of paper. Those eyes of hers haunted him. I knew for a fact that she was waiting for him; Mrs. Cummings confessed it to me in one of her letters that John knew nothing about. When I tried to convince him that Red had gone back to Maine to finish school and planned to move to Kansas when she finished to wait for him to come home, he just smiled his brokenhearted smile and shook his head.

"Don't make me hope for a fairytale; we know it doesn't work that way," John had said. I wanted to show him the letter, prove it to him that it was there in black-and-white, but I couldn't do that. No matter how close you are, "I'm in love with your mom" is never easy to say and it's even harder to let him read a letter corresponding with said mother.

"Yeah, mail would be nice," was the only response I could give. I stood up from my bunk and pulled my pants on. Everything on this blasted island was covered in sand, even my clothes that were kept in my trunk at the end of my bed. Fucking tiny particles got everywhere, even impossible places. I hurriedly finished getting dressed and shoved my shirt into my pants before tightening my belt. John hated waiting for me; I knew he liked to be punctual and get to the breakfast line early. I didn't really care when we got to the line; either way we would get the same small ration as all the other Marines, and every ration would undoubtedly be covered in sand. John disagreed and insisted that we get in line early because the food was "fresher." I didn't know what he was talking about; there was no fresh food, just food with less sand. There was no escape from it. Fucking sand.

May 1941

"Come on, Ben. This is all meant to build character and make us better Marines," John reassured me in his relentlessly optimistic way. He was never optimistic a day in his life until we went to boot camp. Now, suddenly, he's filled with a sense of Honor, Courage, and Commitment—just like the flyer promised.

I grunted as I remade my bed for the third time that morning. The sergeant claimed that being a good marine started with making your bed. I thought it started with a gun, but what did I know? But if that son-of-a-bitch asked me to make it a fourth time, I'd show him that being a good marine started with a right hook.

"I don't get what kinda character I'm meant to be buildin' with straight corners on my blanket, John. If I wanted to make beds I could have stayed in Kansas. At least then I'd be gettin' paid for my work. There, now would ya look at that? Perfect, isn't it?" I stood back and admired my work, comparing it to John's always perfect cot beside mine.

"The left corner is off, you need to straighten the seam or he'll make you do it again," John pointed out, crossing his arms over his chest.

I cursed under my breath and bent over, straightening the goddamn seam. John said that, "when it comes to being knightly, the Marines carry the sword." I think John got his facts wrong, there was nothing knightly about what we were doing.

"Hurry up, Ben. We have to get to PT," John grumbled.

I finished making my bed and glared at him. "There. It's fuckin' perfect now. Let's go before we have to run another five miles like last time."

John shook his head at me but led the way out of the barracks. "That was because you got snarky with the sergeant, keep your mouth shut this time and we'll be fine."

I glared at John as I followed him to the circuit course. He should have known by now that it was impossible for me to keep my mouth shut.

◆ ◆ ◆

"I told you to keep your mouth shut," John scolded me, as we crossed the third mile marker.

"Yeah, ya did, but you knew I wasn't going to listen," I panted, doing my best to keep form and stay in pace with John, who seemed like he was barely breaking a sweat. "Besides, it's not like you needed to try and take the heat for me, you coulda been finished with the course by now and preparing your rations for the Crucible."

John chuckled. "No way was I letting you get yourself in more trouble by quitting early or pulling some other sly shit. We're in this together, like the knights we are."

I huffed and groaned at John. "We aren't kids anymore, you don't have to keep me in line," I panted.

"Ha! That's a damn lie. I keep hoping one of these days you're going to learn, Ben. How many times do you need to get your ass kicked before you think something through and open that trap of yours?"

John's tone reminded me of my father's and I wanted to tackle him to remind him that he wasn't my old man. Instead, I shrugged and kept running. "At least one more time," I smirked and sped up, passing John on the left.

October 1941

"I don't know why ya think there's sand in everythin', Ben. I've never tasted any in my food," Bill said, shaking his head at me from across the table. Bill was a large man from Nebraska whom John and I had received the pleasure of meeting when we were assigned to be in the same unit as him. He was a good six feet, seven inches and at least 245 pounds, and he was the oldest one in our unit at twenty-seven. Apparently he was fond of playing football back home, and even though John disagreed with me and gave me a scolding look when I mentioned it, I thought good ol' Bill had taken a few too many footballs to the head in his Nebraska days. If he didn't have some brain trauma from that sport, then there was no excuse for his ridiculous comment. No sand—what a dumbass.

"That's because ya eat so fast I'm surprised ya taste anythin' ya shovel into that wide trap of yours," I said, watching Bill shovel another forkful into his mouth. The wind picked up, and I felt the tiny granules land on my exposed neck. Bill stared at me.

"Well gosh, Ben, I'm sorry that I'm not a fuckin' princess like you that has to pick at their food and eat one bean at a time. Oh, and don't ya forget the proper way of holdin' that fork: pinky out," Bill said, debonairly lifting his fork and sticking out his fat pinky finger to illustrate his point. Gary and Dan began laughing uproariously, and even John cracked a smirk. I batted my eyelashes like the broads in the films and widened my eyes.

"Well, sugar blossom, it seems you've been practicin'. I'd say your technique is perfect." I slowly put a single bean into my mouth and crunched down. Fucking sand.

"I've been tryin' to impress ya, yer highness; I'm so glad ya noticed. Maybe later, you can show me how to take a piss sittin' down." Bill winked at me and kept eating like an English dame with his fat pinky sticking out.

I had to smile at that one. I leaned back a little on the wooden bench. "I'm sure—"

A gruff and booming voice interrupted me midsentence. "Ladies!" Immediately the five of us stood to attention. Captain Michaels stood stiffly before us, his gray hair perfectly combed. His uniform was pressed and crisp to perfection, and he was eyeing us with the expected level of superior disdain. Gary had suggested that every captain had to take a class on how to be repulsed by the privates before he could be promoted. I'd told him that they just had to be fat-heads in order to be promoted. "I have a special task for you today. Instead of continuing the construction for the airstrip, today your section is going to be responsible for cleaning and reassembling all six five-inch coastal artillery guns. It is important that they are clean and operable," he said, stressing the last word and casting a pointed look in my direction. Oh sure, you break one rifle and they never let up!

"Private Cummings, you will head up this task and make sure that everything is done to my full expectations," Captain Michaels said. "I will be inspecting each one after you complete your task." He stared each one of us down with his beady eyes. There were distinguishable wrinkles around those steely orbs—wrinkles that would appear to be the product of smiling and an overindulgence in laughter. Instead of softening his glare, the wrinkles only functioned to add a forceful frame for it.

"Sir, yes sir!" The five of us said in chorus.

His thin, pale lips twitched a little. He was pleased with his inarguable power, and guys like him got off on power. I bet in five minutes he was jerking off in his tent to get rid of his power-induced erection. He gave a curt nod before stiffly turning and stomping away. I shook my head as I watched him go.

"Well, men, let's finish up and get to it. It'll take all day to clean those guns," Gary said with a groan. Poor kid. Gary was one of the smallest guys I'd seen in the Marines yet, but he sure was a hard worker. He was only about five feet, seven inches and was maybe a hundred twenty pounds. He looked like a little kid with his small frame, reddish-blond hair, bright eyes, and a boyish grin that took up half his face. Gary was the youngest of our unit at seventeen years of age, but he had a sharp wit and was incredibly intelligent. Thank god John finally had another bookworm to talk to so he could stop pestering me about Frederick Nietzsche and the like; I didn't really give a rat's ass about what Zarathustra had to say, but Gary did, since he went to one of those fancy East Coast prep schools. John nodded at Gary and sat down to quickly finish his breakfast.

"Think you're capable of that, Benjamina?" Bill said, prodding me in the stomach with his elbow. I smiled and took my seat to resume eating.

"Didn't your mother ever teach ya it's wrong to abuse a woman, Bill? I think you've gone and bruised me with that trunk ya call an arm." I pouted theatrically and cradled my ribs.

"Don't be so sensitive, princess," he said through a mouthful of potatoes.

"You're just jealous." I smiled toothily at Bill. The other men looked at me confusedly. Bill raised an eyebrow and shoved another forkful between his thin, wide lips.

"I'm jealous of yer sensitivity?" he asked hesitantly. I shook my head and ate a bite of my own food.

"No, ya idiot! You're jealous of my beauty." I brushed the sides of my hair down and batted my lashes again. John and the boys began laughing. Dan socked me in the upper arm and knocked my fork away from my mouth, flinging the potato that was on it into the sand.

"Yer beauty?" Dan said between deep, hearty bellows of laughter. "Ha! Youse got a face that only a mother could love!" Dan loved laughing, and even his laughter was laced with a thick, New Jersey accent. He wasn't as large as Bill, but he was a good size— about the same size as John and me, but wider, and boy was that guy hairy. He had thick black hair on his head, and I bet that if he forgot to shave in the morning he'd have a beard by the time the lunch horn blew. His arms were thick and covered in coarse black hair that matched his three o'clock shadow on his big, square jaw. Talk about a face only a mother could love; Dan had a big, long nose with large

14

nostrils and bushy eyebrows that covered his eyes. John snickered and finished eating his breakfast.

"Oh, and they do love it, those mothers," I said. "In fact, your mother was admiring it the night before we shipped off, Dan-o." Dan lunged playfully at me and got me in a headlock. I stole a glance at John, my laughter coming out somewhat awkwardly; a part of me was wishing I hadn't made that particular joke. John just had a faint smile on his lips but didn't seem bothered by my jest. Dan and I wrestled in the sand until he pinned me down with my arms twisted behind me and had my face pressed into the warm sand. Fucking sand.

"All right, men, let's hop to it!" said John. "Gary's right; we have a lot of them coastal guns to clean."

I let out a sigh and spit out some sand when Dan climbed off of my back.

"Fun's over, princess. Let's get to work." Dan held out a hand to help me up. I grabbed his calloused palm and pulled myself up, watching the sand flow off of my uniform like Niagara Falls. I shook my head and began dusting myself off as we started off toward the supply shed to get our tools.

Fucking sand.

September 1930

Leaves fell from the trees as our swords clanged together in a battle of epic proportions. John and I ran about his yard, chasing each other while brandishing our wooden swords made from branches that were too thin to become good firewood.

"I'll get you this time, you rapscallion! No one defeats Sir Lancelot!" John howled, charging toward me with an intimidating battle cry. I leapt away from him, hitting him with my cardboard shield as I dodged his strike. He made an "oomph" as he fell forward with his momentum, but he swung around and hit his sword against my back. I let out a fierce cry and fell to my knees, lowering my ground so that John could take the death blow upon me.

"What are you boys doing?" a sweet voice asked.

We looked up from our pretend to see Mrs. Cummings standing on the front porch, hands on her hips and a wide smile on her cherry lips. She must have just got back from her job as a telephone operator in town, for her sunny blonde curls were slightly mussed from the large headphones she wore.

"Just playing King Arthur, Mam," John said, standing up and lowering his sword.

Mrs. Cummings pretended to swoon. "What a gallant pair of knights you boys make. You've got your reliable swords and shields, too. Just like real knights in shining armor," she encouraged.

John lit up and a wide smile spread across his features. "Will you play with us? You'll be the fair lady we have to save."

Mrs. Cummings' smile softened, and her eyes lit up with that same kind of energy that John had. "I would love that," she nodded her head, her curls bouncing.

John beamed and turned to me, helping me off the ground. "You'll be my squire, Ben. Together, we'll rescue the fair lady from the fire-breathing dragon!" John led the way of our quest, weaving in and out of the thin trees near the property while fighting off imaginary obstacles with ease. We heard his mother on the porch, dramatically playing her part and calling out for a heroic knight to save her from this dragon.

We pushed our way through the enchanted forest, squirmed our way through the vast desert, and finally stood before the dragon's lair. "I'll save you!" John shouted, brandishing his sword and looking to me to cover his back as he charged. I gave him a nod and held up my shield, ready to cover him from the rain of fire. With a war cry, John leapt forward, slashing and stabbing his way up the porch steps while I kept my shield raised.

He pretended to lose his sword in the battle and Mrs. Cummings let out a well-timed gasp. "Squire! I need aid!" John shouted to me. I bolted to him and gave him my sword so that he could finish defeating the dragon. It was always John's fantasy to be a valiant knight, it wasn't mine. I never minded allowing him to take the victory and save the day.

It was an epic battle with an imaginary opponent that raged before our eyes as Mrs. Cummings and I stood off to the side and watched. As the sun began to set and the evening sky turned pink, John dealt the final blow and slayed the dragon. He turned to his mother, a proud, fatigued smile on his face. "I saved you, Mam. We can go now," he reached out his hand to her and started to lead her down the steps.

Just as their feet reached the ground, a truck door slammed and Mrs. Cummings' face fell. "Thanks, Johnny. You're my little hero," she gave him a kiss on his forehead and ran back up the stairs.

I heard distant shouting from inside the house and pots banging frantically together. I looked over at John, his smile now gone. In its place he wore a stony expression, his eyes staring down at the stick in his hand. He gripped it tighter and turned it into the light. I wondered if he saw the wood gleam like steal when he did that, but just as a glass shattered inside the house he dropped the stick to the ground and squared his shoulders.

"I'll see you tomorrow, Ben," he whispered, climbing the stairs to the Dragon's lair and closing the door behind him, leaving me standing alone with his discarded armor in the fading evening light.

October 1941

As boys John and I used to love playing down by the lake. We would strip down to our skivvies and leap into the brown water, letting it cool our tiny bodies. We would squish the sand between our toes and build castles in the mud on the shore. The sand was different then; at that age it was soft and exotic. Each tiny granule was unique and precious to a landlocked state, and we worshiped the particles as they stuck to our wet bodies. We would carve moats into the sand and mud and fill them with lake water, making our mud castle complete in its fortitude. Then, we would grab sticks and rush the mud castle, fighting the dragon that protected it. We would spear, jab, and stab at it until the dragon fell and the mud castle was nothing more than a blob on the ground; a ghost of its former walls and shape. We never pretended that we had any weapon other than a sword. A rifle never entered our young minds unless we were looking at the one John's father kept mounted on the wall in the den; that rifle belonged to a raging Dragon, and we didn't dare touch it.

After we stormed the mud castle and defeated the dreaded dragon, John and I would lie down in the shapeless remains of the fortress and let the sun slowly dry the beads of water on our skin. I miss that sun.

◆ ◆ ◆

The sun on Wake Island was intense and penetrated my uniform like flames. There was minimal shade on the island, and where the coastal artillery guns were located on the beach there was none, the trees having been cleared out for the pits that would house the monstrous guns. It took three hours to take apart, clean, and reassemble one gun. We all paused in our work to salute the flag as it was raised every morning, and we listened to "To the Colors" proudly. Alvin Waronker was the one in charge of making the bugle call every morning, but he never seemed to get it quite right.

"Gosh, he just struggles at that middle part, don't he?" Bill said when the call was over. I nodded in agreement and turned to get back to work.

"Oh like you could do any better, ya oaf," Dan said, pushing Bill roughly as he passed him to get to another gun. Gary ignored the conversation and just stared helplessly down at the task at hand.

"There's no way we're gonna finish this before we need to get to the airstrip," Gary said with a moan. I completely agreed, but considering the look that John gave him, I bit my tongue and lowered my head; I was in no mood for a lecture, especially not one of John's long-winded, noble lectures. John was usually rather quiet; he always preferred to listen to the stories and conversations of others rather than participating, but give him a cause and a sense of leadership and he could talk your ear off. At the end of it you'd feel inspired to either punch him or conquer the world. Gary caught John's look and simply dropped his shoulders and continued to rub his dirty rag over a piece of the gun.

I looked up toward the blue sky and searched for rain clouds that might cover the greedy sun for some relief, but there were none along the horizon. I glanced over at John and noticed that he, too, had a far-off look in his eyes as he scanned the ocean. I'd caught him doing it before, but I'd never been able to figure out what exactly he was searching for. Enemy ships? The mainland? Storm clouds? An explanation for why he was standing there looking at an ocean of water instead of an ocean of fields? Maybe each day he searched for something new on that unyielding span of blue. All I could be sure of was that he never found it, whatever it was he searched for.

"Ya know why we have to clean these stinkin' guns, don't ya, Gary?" I asked, and I turned to my small friend, who paused in his rubbing to watch me. I gently tilted the mechanical piece I held in my hands to the side so that a river of earthy particles could rush out. Gary started laughing, it was the laugh of a little boy, and he shook his head at me.

"God, Benjamina, you and the fuckin' sand."

I smiled. The exhausted air around us wasn't feeling so heavy any more.

"It's takin' over," I replied seriously.

"Just let it go! It's only sand," Gary said. He tilted the piece in his hand and watched the particles pour out. John smiled at us and lifted his eyes from the machine part that his calloused, square hands were cleaning.

"You know, Ben, I remember a time when you loved the sand," John said, his thin, pink lips pulled back across his teeth in a grin that made him look like the young twenty-two-year-old he was. I made a face at John, scrunching up my nose in disgust at the thought of ever liking sand. John just laughed at my face and nodded.

"Oh yes you did! We would build sand castles for hours down by the lake, and you absolutely loved it! I remember one summer when we were seven or eight that you asked me every damn day if we could go build castles."

"That may be true, but that sand was different," I said. John furrowed his brow and shared a confused look with Gary.

"How was it different, Ben? Sand has the same composition regardless of location. That's why it's all classified as sand." I was glad that prep school in North Carolina had really paid off for Gary.

"Composition doesn't matter, Gary. The sand back home was more respectful," I said, and I began cleaning another part.

John just laughed and shook his head. "How can sand be respectful?" he shouted at me incredulously.

I glared at the granules that slid out of the part in my hand when I tipped it over. "That sand knew where it belonged, and it stayed there," I said, scrubbing my rag over the metal. The guys started howling at that one, stopping in their work to lift their heads to the sky and belt out a hearty laugh.

"Princess, you should really stop bein' so bitter toward the fuckin' sand! It's not goin' nowhere," Bill said. He slapped me on the back and went back to polishing the base of the gun.

"Never. Just you wait; this fuckin' sand will rise and consume us all!" I said dramatically. Dan kicked sand at me and made it go down the back of my uniform.

"You's a damn lunatic, Benny boy," said Dan, wiping the sweat that was collecting on his brow with the back of his forearm.

John looked on and laughed as he watched me wiggle and dance in attempt to get the sand out. "Always the damn theatrics with you, Ben," he playfully scolded. "Can't take anything seriously."

November 1940

We walked in silence, the Dragon's lair shrinking behind us until there was nothing but trees and fields. I stared up at my great heroes and waited for John to say something.

"I couldn't do it," he eventually said after a long silence. I nodded, waiting for him to continue. Usually, if I just waited patiently, John would open up without the need of a push. He let out a deep, defeated sigh and continued walking. I could tell he was sobering up, because his steps were straighter and his skin wasn't quite as flushed. I guess the cool autumn air had managed to bring him back to his senses. I waited silently for John to continue, and when he didn't, it occurred to me that this might be one of the rare occasions when he needed a slight push.

"Why not?" I asked innocently, tilting my head back once more to gaze at the stars. I saw John shrug out of my peripheral vision. He remained silent. So did I.

"Hey, Ben?" He asked softly after a while. We were almost back to my house at this point but still trudging along the dirt road between our two homes. I turned my face away from the stars to look at John. His head was bent low, and his hands were stuffed in his jacket pockets.

"Yeah?" I said, unsure of where this was going to go. He didn't lift his head, and he began to kick a small rock down the road, edging it along with each stride that he took.

"We should get out of here," he said finally.

I nodded in agreement and smiled. Our conversations always turned this way after John's numerous attempts to confront the Dragon. "Oh sure. Where do you want to go?" I asked carelessly, turning back to my stars.

"Anywhere," John said resolutely.

I nodded, half listening. "That's a good start. Someday we'll have to sit down and actually plan this great escape of ours." I laughed. John didn't say anything back. I slowly brought my head back down and stared at him. Usually at this point he would eagerly agree, and we would start listing off all the countries that we remembered from school. He would say the name of somewhere exotic, like South Africa; I would counter with something ridiculous, like Milwaukee. His silence this time began to concern me, and I started to slow my pace beside him. Eventually I came to a complete stop and waited for him to turn and look at me. When John finally realized I was no longer walking beside him, he halted in his rock-kicking and turned toward me. I watched him and could see the gears in his head turning. Try as he might, he could never hide from me.

"I was talking to Ray yesterday; ran into him outside the hardware store. He said he joined the army; said they were going to ship him to Iceland to help with the war." He paused, his eyes darting down to his feet. I nodded, unsure where he was going with this.

"You want to go to Iceland?" I asked, confused. That wasn't exactly exotic. John shook his head with his lips twitching upward into a smile. I frowned at him. Maybe he was still drunk.

"No, I don't want to go to Iceland. Ray was saying there were a lot of places that the military would ship you to help our country and be honorable." He said this softly, insecurely almost. He brought his eyes toward mine again, and I suddenly had an idea where he was taking this.

"Honorable?" I asked, hoping that he hadn't already planned our great escape without me. I was hoping even more that if he had planned it out, it didn't involve me getting shot at.

"Yeah, we could be soldiers! Just like real knights!" He said with excitement, the insecurity gone. My jaw dropped as I watched John's typically stoic face split into a rare grin that showed all of his white teeth and lit up his blue eyes. He took a few eager steps toward me, resembling the boy I grew up with. "They have a branch called the Marines! They even have swords in their uniform! Just like real knights!"

I watched in shock and horror as John grabbed my hands like a schoolgirl, that energy of his just wrapping around me and pulling me in. I shook my head against it.

"We could be real knights, Ben," he said pleadingly, his eyes filled with a hope and desperation that I'd never seen before. I frowned at him, knowing I was going to give in even though I didn't want to. I didn't want to be honorable; I knew that being honorable usually got you killed, or at least missing a few vital limbs or something.

"I'm not a knight, John," I said, hoping he'd forget about it once he was sober. I could tell from the clearness of his eyes that he was already sober, but I had no other explanation for this wild idea if it wasn't generated by large amounts of booze.

John smiled wider at me, his grip tightening around my frozen hands. "Ah! But where would a knight be without his squire?" he asked enthusiastically. He let go of my hands and took a step back, waiting for my answer.

I narrowed my eyes at him. "What do you really know about the Marines?" I asked, trying to find any kind of flaw in this cockamamie plan.

"I picked up some pamphlets yesterday after talking to Ray. They're stationing a bunch of them in the Pacific!" John replied eagerly.

I shook my head again, wishing I was the one intoxicated instead of him. "But why the Marines!" I shouted.

John smiled at me, his eyes lighting up and that energy of his just drawing me in. "Because they carry the sword," he replied easily. I knew there was no escaping it. Not that night anyway.

"Why don't we talk more about this in the morning?" I said, hoping that in the morning it would be an empty thought that dissolved with the alcohol in his veins. I walked past John, successfully ending the conversation knowing that the next time he brought it up, I was going to agree.

October 1941

We were reclining in the dining hall; our empty trays sat idly on the table. We had completed our assignment and had managed to clean all of the coastal artillery guns in time to get to our job building the airstrip. It wasn't our team's night to be on watch duty, so we had the remaining hour to ourselves before we had to retire to our bunks. Dan and Bill were playing a game of gin. Gary was busy writing a love letter to his sweetheart back home in North Carolina, and John was silently reading a book. I watched John's eyes scan the inked words on the pages, amazed at how entranced he was. John had only packed three books, and he had read this book so many times I knew he had most of it memorized. I turned my head away from John and stared up at the night sky. I listened to the turning of pages in John's chronicle of King Arthur and his knights; I listened to the slap of cards as they were drawn from the deck and then discarded; I listened to the scratching of a pen on letter paper, oozing declarations and sentiments with each blot of ink. My eyes automatically searched for familiar constellations—Andromeda, Perseus, Orion—and they gleamed and shined down at me. My eyes stared unblinkingly at the sky, relieved that at least they were unchanging.

"That book's going to fall apart the way you keep reading it, Cummings," a mocking voice said, interrupting the silence. I turned my head away from the stars and looked toward the voice, which had come from a figure standing behind John. His lips were pulled back from his teeth in a slight sneer, his dark eyes squinting unflatteringly in friendly disdain. John gently set his book down on the table and stood up to face the other marine.

"Jim, what brings you over to our table?" John asked socially. Jim tilted his head up a little so that he could look John in the eye. Jim wasn't a short man; he was the same height I was at six feet. But John was taller than Jim by about four inches, and it was obvious that those four inches were four inches of discomfort for Jim.

"Just passing through," said Jim. "Thought I might congratulate your team on a good day of housework; those guns sure are shiny now." His eyes twinkled with satisfaction at his insult.

John smiled back into those dark eyes; his radiant energy was shining through his teeth. "Thanks, Jim. My team and I appreciate you noticing our hard work. I couldn't help but notice that your team did a mighty fine job today as well." Jim's lips slowly began to curve downward from the tilted smirk they had been in.

"I've never seen such fine trenches before; your boys certainly know how to dig," John said, slowly crossing his arms over his gray T-shirt and smiling in satisfaction at Jim. Jim glared at John while the silent tension in the room escalated. I let out a deep breath and rolled off the bench I was lying on. Neither one of them turned to look at me as I approached; they continued to stare hatefully at each other.

"He's right, Jim; them trenches for the airstrip are mighty beautiful," I said. "I just loved the way your boys piled the sand, a real work of art." I smiled broadly at Jim and swung my arm around John's shoulders. Jim pulled his lips back and clenched his teeth, his eyes narrowing threateningly.

"I don't believe I was addressing you, Halpert," said Jim, "but then again, your head is so far up Cummings's ass I should know by now that I can't talk to him without getting your idiotic input too."

I smiled toothily and stood up straighter with mock pride. "Oh, ya know just how to sweet-talk me, Jim. It's okay, though." I comfortingly put my hand that wasn't around John's shoulders on Jim's shoulder; he abruptly knocked it off with contempt.

"It's okay, because I know that behind your disgust, you really admire my dazzling input. I know, I know, you want to learn my ways. Sadly, I don't think it's possible to make you less of a dumbass," I said with a wink at Jim.

Bill and Dan burst out laughing behind me, and John did his best to contain his chuckles. Jim let out a feral growl, and as he swung a fist at my proud smile, it occurred to me that I might've gone too far. His fist connected with my jaw, and I collapsed onto John from the force of it. Some guys just can't take a joke. Before either of us could regain ourselves, Jim pulled me off of John and sent a blow to my gut. Jim really needed to get a sense of humor. I sputtered and gasped for air, trying to calculate my next move. Jim took a step back and made ready to punch my bowed head, but before I could charge him, John stepped in front of me and grabbed Jim's fist. Bill came up from behind Jim and pinned his arms behind his back. Gary ran up to me and helped me stand up while Dan took a protective stance beside John. Jim looked from John to Dan and then back at Gary and me; his teeth were bared in anger, and his dark hair was sprawled across his forehead, but he didn't fight Bill's hold.

John leaned forward into Jim's face, his long nose nearly touching Jim's. "It would be wise for you to walk away now, private," John hissed. Jim's breathing slowly calmed, and he gave John a terse nod, his eyes never looking away from John's eyes, which were tinged with animosity. Bill slowly released Jim, who smartly didn't put up a fight. Jim stood proudly and straightened his uniform. He nodded again at John and moved past him, sending a sinister glare in my direction as he walked past.

We waited in silence for a couple of minutes, making sure that Jim had retired from our area completely, before John spun around and stared at me. His eyes were still tinged with anger, and his lips were pressed in a stern, firm line. Dan and Bill quickly returned to their card game, and Gary scampered back to his letter writing, their heads all hung low and inconspicuous. I watched them all leave before meeting John's unwavering gaze. I smiled at John; my lip split a little from Jim's punch, and blood oozed into my mouth. John continued to stare at me.

"You're an idiot," John said through clenched teeth. I shrugged my shoulders in agreement and nodded.

John shook his head. "You've got to stop pushing people's buttons; one of these days you're going to do it and I won't be around to stop them from pummeling your ass." John gave me a glare and then pushed past me to continue reading his book.

I shook my head and smiled. "You're a knight, John. Of course you'll always be there." I muttered to myself. I wiped the blood off my lip, walked back to my bench, lay down, and once again turned my attention to the stars.

◆ ◆ ◆

Jim sure was an interesting sort; a real moron, but an interesting one at least. He was a couple years older than John and me, but based off of his maturity level, you'd guess he was barely out of grade school let alone twenty-four years old. He'd been stationed at Wake Island since August, when they established the permanent garrison, and he had made it quite clear when we arrived that we weren't welcome unless we were groveling at his well-shined boots. Well, you know that didn't sit well with John. John didn't grovel to anyone, and when someone disrespected him and his squire, then all his knightly rules went out the window. Needless to say, we were never gonna be close to Jim.

Luckily, we were in different sections; otherwise, there might've been some real problems. Our platoon was in charge of Battery L, and Jim's platoon was a part of the aviation personnel. I'll admit I was kind of jealous that Jim got to fly the F4F-3 Wildcats, but if being stationed on the beach meant I didn't have to see his ass-face, then I was happy. That's not to say that I didn't manage to get into any trouble with him; I'd gotten into countless brawls with Jim because I just couldn't keep my mouth shut and he just couldn't control his temper: not a good combination to mesh together. John was always there to get me out of it, though. He'd jump in and keep Jim from breaking my ribs, or my arms—but not my nose … he always came after that. You'd think that it would've upset me that I couldn't take Jim on my own and that I always needed John's help, but it really didn't. Sure, most guys would've been sore about it, but John always had my back. That's not to say I'd never taken a guy down before; I did it all the time in school. Jim fought dirty, though. It was never just me and him fighting; it was me, him, and his stupid groupies. I was a decent fighter, don't get me wrong, but four against one wasn't exactly at my skill level.

But it was at John's skill level. John had been fighting off beasts his whole life. He was one of the best fighters I'd ever met, yet he only fought if it was to save my sorry ass. I guess a valiant knight couldn't allow his squire to come to shame, or to become a beaten bloody pulp at the unworthy hands of Jim and his goons.

July 1931

"Please stop hitting him! Please stop!" Mrs. Cummings screamed, tears running down her beautiful cheeks, leaving black streaks of mascara on her white face. Her red lips kept opening and closing around desperate pleas. The Dragon just raised his fist and brought it down again on the small, bowed head in front of him. The boy was on his knees, his arms shaking to support his frame under the bashes. Mrs. Cummings ran toward the Dragon and grabbed his raised arm in an attempt to stop another blow from hitting her son. John raised his bleeding head and peered at the scene from under a screen of shaggy blond hair.

"Get off!" The Dragon said, and he slapped Mrs. Cummings with his other hand, sending her sprawling across the kitchen floor. John let out a feral growl in his throat and attempted to push himself up.

"Stay down! That fucking whore isn't worth defending!" the Dragon yelled. He lifted his foot and smashed it against John's hunched back. Blood ran down John's face and clumped in his hair from the cracks he had taken to his head, and the air was stolen from his lungs when he collapsed on the floor. The Dragon lifted his foot again to deliver it to the same spot on John's back, but it instead connected with the delicate ribs of Mrs. Cummings.

"Get out of my way, bitch!" The Dragon screamed as Mrs. Cummings wrapped herself around John's crumpled form. The Dragon swung his fist at her head.

31

"That's enough!" a stern voice yelled. A firm hand grabbed the Dragon's wrist and thrust it behind his back. "You're under arrest!" The Dragon attempted to struggle against the strong arms that held him captive, but the sheriff was stronger and pushed him out the door. The town doctor and a nurse rushed inside to tend to Mrs. Cummings and her twelve-year-old son.

"She fucking deserved it!" The Dragon said, growling. The sheriff pushed him down the back stairs toward the police car waiting on the back road. I stood beside the stairs, watching as the Dragon was thrust into the backseat of the car. I glared ruthlessly at the Dragon. He must've felt my hatred toward him, because he turned and looked at me in my spot of semidarkness beside the stairs. His lips curled around his sharp teeth when he saw me. The car began to drive off, and as it passed me along the road, the Dragon did something that sent chills through my body and into the marrow of my bones: he smiled. His teeth gleamed in the dim porch light, and his lips oozed pride and contempt.

I felt a rough hand on the top of my shaggy brown hair and looked up to see my father watching the car drive away. He patted my head and let his hand slide into his coat pocket, his gaze remaining on the road ahead. "It's a good thing you came and got us, son. I'm proud of you for doin' the right thing." He smiled down at me, the lines on his face accentuated by the dim glow emanating from the porch light. He let out a deep sigh and scratched at his thick, well-trimmed beard. "I'd better go in and take a statement from Mrs. Cummings about how this all started. You go on home and let your mother know I won't be home for dinner tonight." I nodded up at my father, who gave me another smile and pat on my head before turning around and ascending the stairs into the Dragon's lair.

February 1940

"Benjamin Halpert! You will be a gentleman and escort your sister and Mrs. Crow's niece about town this evening, and I don't want to hear any more protests from you," my mother scolded, folding the laundry and tossing it into the basket as she harshly pulled the clothes from the line.

I groaned and leaned against the door, running my hands through my hair which had gotten too long again. "John and I were going to go get some booze and meet some broads," I countered, trying to get out of having to spend my first night off with my younger sister and some Yank visiting her aunt from her fancy college school in Maine.

My mother put her hands on her hips, her fingers clutching around the shirt in her hand making it wrinkle. She glared at me as only a mother could and I winced, knowing I was going to have to do what she said. "Now see here young man, that's no way to talk about a lady. You are twenty-years-old and I don't care much for your being a drugstore cowboy while drinking that giggle water. Any girl you meet doing that is bound to be a flour-loving floozy. That's no kind of girl to marry,"

I rolled my eyes and crossed my arms over my chest. "No one talks like that anymore, Mam. 'Sides, there aren't any floozies in this town."

"Well those still aren't the kinds of girls you ought to be associating with. I know Betty Miller's daughter is all pretty now

33

that she's grown up, but she is a prime example of the type of flour-lover I don't want you ending up with. That girl is caked in makeup and it's not becoming."

I opened my mouth to argue more, but she cut me off before I could utter a sound.

"Now go make yourself presentable, brush your hair and straighten your shirt. You're going with your sister and Mrs. Crow's niece and that's the end of it. Understood?"

I lowered my eyes and nodded my head. "Yes, ma'am."

My mother grinned and resumed folding the laundry. "Good, now why don't you bring John along with you and you can both be sturdy gentlemen like I raised you to be," she gave me a pointed look and I nodded, knowing I had lost this round— and probably any other one we might have in the future about it.

◆ ◆ ◆

I rubbed my hands together, trying to spark some warmth in them while John and I waited for my sister to come out with Mrs. Crow's niece. They had been in the house gabbing for hours—at least it felt like hours. My toes were numb and my fingers weren't far behind. I glanced over to John and he just stood beside me stoically, that ever-present stony expression on his face. It was like the cold didn't bother him at all. Maybe he was stone.

"What is takin' them so damn long?" I asked, trying to peek in the windows to see what they were up to.

John shrugged and stuffed his hands farther in his pockets. So he did feel the cold, after all.

"Dunno, girls always take forever gabbing away and the like. Where did your sis say we were taking them?" John shuffled his feet a little and then resumed his stillness.

"Who knows? I wasn't listenin'. She rambles on so damn fast," I replied, cutting myself off as the front door opened. My sister stepped out first, her hat low on her head to block the cold. Following close behind her was one of the prettiest girls I'd ever seen. Mrs. Crow wasn't exactly a looker, so I never expected her niece to be such a cookie.

She waved good-bye to her aunt and tossed her long red hair over her shoulder. Her skin was white as the snow that fell around us. I swear she must have been related to Snow White in another life; if it hadn't been for her hair, I'd say she was the very same princess. She was tall and swanky; her cupid-bow lips curved into the prettiest smile, her teeth shining with superiority. Red shivered a little in the cold air, but her smile stayed strong and pleasant.

"Scarlet, this is my brother Ben, and our family friend John," my sister politely introduced. I shook her hand and was surprised by the grip she had. This was no shy damsel, it was no wonder none of the other men in town had swooped her up yet. One glance at her and they knew she was out of this town's league; their dicks went limp and shrunk with just a wave and a smile from her as they cowered from the beauty. If Red had been my type, I would have been no exception. As it was, I preferred blondes over redheads and was spared from any humiliating attempt I might have made to pick her up. I glanced over at John and wasn't surprised to see the admiration in his eyes. That energy of his flared and wrapped around all of us and I knew, he was a goner. John was too stupid, or maybe just too proud to admit that someone was better that him—and Red was better than the lot of us by far.

"Pleasure to meet you, Miss," John greeted with the first smile I'd seen from him in over six months, shaking her hand delicately. His eyes held onto hers, sparkling with that unique energy that belonged solely to him, and her smile widened. With that one smile, and without any competition to speak of, I watched John steal himself the heart of a pretty college princess.

October 1941

We had retired to our bunks soon after the incident with Jim. John and the boys agreed, of course, not to notify the captain about the mishap. It'd be my luck that if they had, I would've been the one doing dishes and kitchen duty for the next month, not that ass-bag, Jim. So we just kept our mouths shut and carried on about our lives pretending that I wasn't bleeding from the nose; it was an elegant system we had, really.

Once Dan and Bill had finished their card game, the gambling fiends that they were, and Gary got all teary-eyed when he read over his letter, we decided to part ways and go to our tents. Dan and Bill shared a bunk together and had done so for the past two years that they had been enlisted in the Marines. Prior to being stationed on Wake Island, the two of them were stationed over on Oahu, where there was more than just sand. They had told us stories about what Hawaii looked like and what the town life was like. When they weren't on duty and were able to get off base, they'd sneak into the town and have a few beers with some very lovely locals. It was always a hoot and a half to listen to some of their stories. Bill had more stories, as he was twenty-eight and had been in the Marines for over six years now; but Dan had quite a few considering he still had three years of the Marines on John, Gary, and me.

Some nights they'd talk about all the crazy things they'd done or seen while on or off duty and we'd all have a laugh. Some of the stories weren't humorous, and when Dan or Bill told those stories, we'd all sit quietly for a spell before one or both of them would get up from the table and go their own way. Bill would usually go for a walk, and Dan would typically go check in with the privates that were on watch duty.

Gary was like a kid; then again, he basically was a kid at his age. He would always listen intently to Bill's and Dan's stories as if they were literary heroes or something. You should've seen the way his face would light up when Dan would talk about the time he was necking with some girl outside of a bar and her dad just happened to be walking out of that same bar with a bunch of his equally displeased friends. Oh, when Dan would get to the part where her dad spotted the two of them and took a swing at Dan, Gary would be on the edge of his seat, bouncing up and down. Gary was still green when he was stationed on Wake Island a month after John and me. He had only been to the cinema once, he'd just graduated from his fancy prep school, and he'd never seen a girl naked, let alone ever touched one. The boys and I were only too happy to help rough Gary up a bit. While we couldn't exactly help him with the whole girl thing, seeing as none of us had any of those body parts and on this sandbar everyone at least claimed to have a dick, we could help him with growing a backbone and getting a little rougher around those edges instead of being so soft. At first he was a little sensitive to our jokes and prods, but eventually he loosened up and began dealing them right back. I was never prouder than the first time I heard that boy loosen his lips and let the word "fuck" fly out of them.

Gary had been bunking by himself until the next shipment of troops came in. His old bunk mate ended up getting his leg blown off by a broken rifle that had been improperly cleaned—they still have no conclusive evidence as to who the neglectful private was that cleaned that particular rifle—and it was shortly after that incident that our unit was moved from rifle inspection to miscellaneous tasks. No idea why.

After the five of us decided to retire to our respective bunks, I lay in my bed a while, waiting to hear the long, heavy breaths that John emitted when he fell into a deep slumber. I am not sure how long I lay there, counting the tiny holes in the canvas tent above my head—I got to seventy-five—before I heard those deep, rhythmic breaths coming from John's lungs. I waited for the count of eight more holes in the canvas before I noiselessly rolled out of my cot. I knelt into the sand, hating the very touch of it against the flesh of my bare knees, and began working the lock on my footlocker at the base of my bed. I stole a look at John to make sure that my antics hadn't disturbed him, because if there was one thing I'd learned about John, it was that he was no heavy sleeper.

John's chest still rose steadily with slumber, so I continued my task. Eventually, I defeated the padlock on my footlocker and opened the chest to search for my buried treasure. I kept the precious commodity hidden from any prying eyes, securely wrapped in a pair of my underwear for protection and disguise and shoved in the back right corner of my footlocker. If anyone had been curious enough to pry into my personal belongings, my treasure was safe, because I knew no one would dare touch another man's underwear. I grabbed the white shorts that were shoved in the back and pulled from them a small stack of letters, carefully bound by a single piece of twine. I took a last glance at the still dreaming John and carefully closed my footlocker, letters in hand. I set the letters on my bed while I pulled on a pair of pants before I stealthily snuck out of the tent. I went to the lunch area, where I knew there would be somewhat sufficient light for me to read by. On the nights when I would feel particularly homesick, I would grab the letters Mrs. Cummings had written me and read them. I loved reading her passionate words written in her slanted scrawl; the elegance with which they were written contradicted the words on the paper. She would usually start her letters with something benign like the weather in Kansas or how Red was doing, since she knew John would never ask her in the letters that he wrote to her. Then, about halfway through, her letters would become far more personal, making me long for her arms. I could just see those blue eyes of hers turning gray with her passion, and her body writhing.

"Halpert, what are you doing away from your tent? I figured you and Cummings enjoyed this time together to suck each other's cocks in private?" It was Jim.

I rolled my eyes and quickly folded my letter back into its envelope. I rose from the wooden bench that I had been sitting on and languorously stretched my arms above my head. I let out a sigh and turned around to finally face his scowl. I swear that man didn't know another facial expression. I smiled politely at him before answering. "Nah, that's why I came lookin' for ya because I know how much you'd like to suck my dick." Sometimes I wondered if all these jokes toward Jim would get me in trouble one day, because he did seem to take an awful keen interest in my sexual activities. Jim's frown deepened, and he took a threatening step toward me. I knew that, since it was late, all of his goons were either on duty or were asleep, which meant that if he started throwing punches, I might have a shot at a fair fight. I continued to smile at Jim until a gentle breeze picked up and blew across the little sandbar called an island, rustling the stack of letters I had sitting on the table. The movement of the paper was enough to catch Jim's attention, and suddenly he was much less interested in me and much more interested in my letters.

"What do you have here, Halpert? Letters from your dear mother back in the middle of nowhere?" He reached out for one of the letters, no doubt so that he could read one and mock my lovely mother. The ass-bag, I thought. How dare he intend to mock my mother! Jim tilted his head to read the name of the sender on the envelope, and I made a quick grab for the stack. I was able to slap his greedy hand away from my letters, but the small smile that tugged at the corner of his lips told me that he had seen the name of the sender and knew full well that they were not from my mother.

"I'd thank ya very much not to invade my privacy. My sex life is one thing, because I know that ya need those images of me so that you can masturbate before ya go to sleep every night, but my family is somethin' ya need not worry your damaged little brain about." I nodded with finality at Jim and moved to walk past him. As I began the trek back to my tent, I heard soft chuckles coming from Jim.

"Sure thing, Halpert; I'm sure your family secrets are very important to maintain."

March 1926

Our feet crunched over the frozen ground, our hands stuffed into our pockets even though I had mittens on. My hands were too warm with the mittens on inside the coat pockets, but I didn't want to draw attention to the fact that John didn't have any. My mother took the time to knit a new pair for my sister and me at the start of winter out of some old rags she had saved, but I knew his mother didn't know how to do the same things my mother did. She sure knew how to embroider lace real pretty, though, not that it did much good now that no one could afford lacy things. John told me once that she was a lady and his grandparents on that side were real Ritzy with lots of dough. He'd never met them, but Mrs. Cummings told him stories.

"You're gonna love it, Ben. He got it a couple months ago," John said, leading me up the porch steps to his house. It was smaller than my house, but not by much. The Cummings had more land than us, and in Kansas that was worth a lot more than a few more feet on the great room.

"He won't mind us lookin' at it, will he?" I hesitated at the door, watching John walk in and poke around for his folks.

He grinned at me, signaling the coast was clear and shook his head. "Nah, he'll never know." He waved me in and that was all the encouragement I needed. John led me over to the far wall, behind the dining table on the other side of their great room. We stood there and stared in awe at it. The afternoon sun, low in the winter sky, glistened off the polished wood and iron sight.

"Wow, now that's mighty keen," I gushed. I'd never seen a rifle half as nice. "The one my daddy's got isn't anywhere near this fancy. He keeps it in the shed, he hates them rabbits that eat the sprouts in the field," I ramble, wanting to reach up and slide my fingers over the walnut and 24-inch barrel.

"It's a Winchester Model 1890. Cost him twenty-two dollars," John said, his eyes gleaming with excitement.

I let out a low whistle. "Twenty-two dollars? Where's he get that kind of dough?" I asked.

John shrugged and stepped over to the long cabinet beneath the rifle. "Work, I guess. He works all the time so he must be doin' something important. Look down here. Here's where he keeps the cartridges. He likes the .22 Longs." John pulled the box of calibers out, lifting one up to show me.

"It's a mighty fine rifle. What's your daddy use it for if it's hanging up in here?" I ask, wondering what kind of small game comes up to their front door. My daddy always has to go into the fields to kill his rabbits.

John shrugs again and puts the cartridges back. "I dunno, I've never seen him use it. I just know he likes to keep it loaded, that's why he told me not to touch it." John looked at the rifle again, his head titling to the side as he considered it with great detail. "It's his favorite thing, mama says he loves it even more than her."

"Your mama's so pretty I don't believe that. Where's she at anyways?" I look around, wondering why Mrs. Cummings wasn't home to greet us like my mother was.

"I dunno. I'm sure she'll be back soon," John whispered.

I pursed my lips and bounced on my toes. "Want to come over to my house? My mom will have snacks ready," I offer. John instantly lit up and nodded with a grin on his face.

"Sure! Let's go." We headed back into the cold toward my house. We chatted along the way, but the whole time I couldn't stop wondering what use that pretty rifle would have inside the house like that.

October 1941

I watched John closely when we ate breakfast that morning, as I had a tendency to do after I read Mrs. Cummings's letters. I wasn't typically a paranoid guy, but I always feared that John wasn't actually asleep and had been watching me the whole time and knew exactly how much I loved his mother. It put me on edge.

"What's up with ya today, Ben? Ya seem more twitchy than usual," Bill said sweetly while shoveling potatoes in his mouth. I just glared at him. How dare he pinpoint my discomfort and draw attention to it!

"I'm not twitchy," I said. "I just didn't sleep well is all." I picked up my fork and inspected the potato on it for sand particles. I just wanted him off my back, and I was not twitchy. Bill just gave me a funny look and shook his head.

"Nah, I agree with Bill," said Dan. "Somethin's definitely up yer ass this mornin', Benny." I just shrugged my shoulders and ate faster, hoping they'd drop it. I made a face when I crunched down on some sand. Fucking sand!

"John catch ya jerking off again?" Dan asked helpfully, nodding his head in John's direction. John looked up from his tray with a shocked and disgusted face.

"Argh! If that was the case, then I'd be the one acting twitchy and traumatized." John gave a dramatic shudder at the thought. Gary started laughing, and his little boy laughter caused the rest of the table to join him; even John let out a few chuckles.

I shook my head and smiled. "Nah, luckily John was still asleep when I finished this time," I said. I laughed at John's disturbed face; his eyes were wary, obviously not sure if I was joking or not, but his lips were still turned up in a dimple-showing smile.

"Well, men, we should get to work on that airstrip. We don't need Captain Michaels ridin' our ass this mornin', not that I'm sure ya wouldn't enjoy it, Ben," Bill said, punching my shoulder when he stood up.

"Well, ya know how much I want Captain Michaels," I rolled my eyes and grabbed my sand-infested breakfast tray. As our troop sauntered away from the dining area, I glanced at John. The smile from earlier still stained his lips, and his step seemed joyous; he still had no idea. As I watched John walk toward the coastal artillery guns, I took a deep breath, and my paranoia was successfully suppressed.

September 1935

"That bastard doesn't deserve to fucking breathe!" John screamed in fury. I just sat on my porch steps as I watched him pace up and down my backyard. I'd never seen John so angry in all my sixteen years of life—ten years of our friendship. He stomped his feet in the dirt and made little clouds of dust form in the still autumn air. I didn't speak to him; I just watched him as he paced back and forth, tense with rage.

"I'm going to take him down! Who the fuck does he think he is?" John shouted vehemently. His eyes had darkened to a stormy resolve; they were piercing in their ferocity and added a terrifying beauty to the hardened face of a gallant knight. John paused in his frenzied pacing and turned toward me. His eyes said, "Grab your sword and shield, I need you," but all that came out of his parted lips was "Come on." I needed no further prodding than that to follow him into battle.

◆◆◆

The afternoon sun was warm on our necks as we trekked toward the Dragon's lair. John's walk was determined and fearless; he was finally going to take down the beast that had tormented him for the past sixteen years of his life. He had frozen back in May, when he had first attempted to take on the Dragon, but now he walked with determination and I knew he was ready. I could almost see the sun glinting off the shiny armor he wore as it permeated through the dense leaves of the trees. His stride was confident and noble; with each step he took, righteousness pumped through his veins. I was still not entirely sure why John needed me to go with him; he'd never let me attack his Dragon. The only rationale I've ever been able to come up with is that he needed his squire to shield his back and bear witness to his triumph—or to carry him home should he fail. When we reached the steps that ascended to the Dragon's dwelling, we paused. I looked over at John and studied him intently. His eyes still held that stormy resolve, and his jaw was tight and square. His shoulders were pushed back, and his muscles were clenched in anticipation. He was ready for battle.

He took the stairs so eagerly that they shook under the weight of him. He paused once more at the screen door, the entrance to where the Dragon lay waiting, and took a deep breath. For a moment, I thought he'd chicken out and we'd walk back to my house in silence. John just shook his head, let out a grunt of determination, and threw the door open with a fierce crack as the wooden frame split under the force.

"What the fuck was that!" I heard from inside. John bared his teeth and stepped over the threshold into the lair. I stood in my customary spot beside the stairs, listening to the commotion coming from inside, just waiting for my cue to intervene. I listened to shouting as John screamed at the Dragon, calling him names like "motherfucker" and "ass twat." I didn't know until then that John was so creative with his cursing. It was so rare to hear him utter an obscenity that it never crossed my mind that he could come up with such phrases. The Dragon began shouting back at him, and it didn't take very long for the first blow to hit. I heard the fist connect with flesh and the groan of pain that came from John. I climbed the stairs and peeked through the screen door, in case I needed to rescue the knight earlier than I anticipated.

John recovered from the hit and swung at his father, his fist connecting with the Dragon's jaw. The Dragon's head snapped to the side from the force, but when he turned back toward John, his eyes were glowing red. I could see John falter a little from the Dragon's piercing eyes; he had never seen them that furious before. John made ready to swing at his father again, but the Dragon caught his fist and thrust it behind John's back. John let out a cry of pain as the Dragon twisted his arm unnaturally until there was a pop and his arm was forced from its socket. John cried out and spun around, swinging his other fist at the Dragon and breaking his nose. Blood poured from the Dragon's face and made his red eyes even more frightening. John pulled back his leg and sent his foot colliding with the Dragon's protruding stomach. The Dragon folded and gasped from the blow. John lifted his leg to kick the Dragon's bent head, but the Dragon charged at John and sent him sprawling on the floor.

The Dragon pushed John down and climbed on top of him so that he couldn't move. He grabbed tufts of John's blond hair and began slamming his head into the hardwood floor of the living room. I saw blood start dripping down John's face, his eyes clenched in pain. I opened the screen door at that moment and darted through the kitchen toward the living room. The Dragon was too busy smashing John's head to notice me, so I used his distraction to my advantage. Adrenaline was pumping heavily through my body, and I could hear it pounding in my ears. I always was an irrational person, very spontaneous and instinctual. I never really thought things through, which had a tendency to complicate situations. I ran to the far wall and grabbed the rifle off of it; I swung it around and aimed it directly at the Dragon's thick skull.

"Let him go!" I shouted, my voice stronger than I expected it to be. My hands were shaking, but I kept my gaze trained on the beast. Time seemed to freeze in that moment: the rifle pointed at the hideous Dragon, John covered in blood, and my heart pounding. In that moment my mind suddenly recalled when John and I were younger and admired the very gun I now held in my quavering hands. Our admiration was superficial compared to the immense power I learned it held. The Dragon stared at me, his red eyes clouded with rage and fear. John opened his eyes a little bit, and from under thick lashes stained with blood, his eyes met mine. That one look from those gentle eyes—no longer hardened or grayed from wrath—made my shaky hands strong, and my breathing slow.

"Let him go," I said again, my voice quiet but stern. The Dragon stared down the barrel and slowly rolled off of John. He sat on his knees and watched me, his red eyes steady and calculating. John slowly tried to lift himself up, his good arm nearly buckling under his weight. I began to lower the gun so that I could go help John, but as soon as I did, the Dragon took his chance and attacked. He pulled a switchblade from his back pocket and, in one swift motion, brought it down toward John's chest. John tried to roll away from the shining blade, but he only succeeded in moving his tired and broken body enough that the blade sunk into the flesh of his shoulder. John let out a groan of agony as the steel pierced his flesh, and I quickly brought the butt of the rifle to my shoulder. Before I even knew what I was doing, my steady finger had pulled back the trigger, and an ear-shattering bang echoed throughout the house.

◆ ◆ ◆

I sat in the waiting room in the hospital with my mother and father, waiting for Mrs. Cummings to come back and update us on John's condition. My father kept asking me what had happened, my mother just cried into her handkerchief, but I just sat there quietly. I couldn't tell my father what had happened, because honestly, even I wasn't completely sure. The adrenaline had created holes in my memory. All I could tell my father was that we had had an encounter with the Dragon, I had stolen his car, and here we were. My father wanted more from me, but I wasn't going to say anything until I had talked to John.

Mrs. Cummings returned from his room, tears running down her pretty face. I remember then looking at her and feeling wretched for my role in the events that caused those gorgeous eyes to water. He was going to be fine, she said. They had set his arm and stitched up the knife wound. He had a concussion, a rather serious one, she told us. She continued to talk about more of the technicalities, but I wasn't listening.

"He wants to see you, Ben," she said. I nodded and got up from my chair slowly, my muscles suddenly hurting. I held her eyes for a moment longer, attempting to see John's condition through them so I could prepare myself, but all she did was smile. Taking a shaky breath in, I turned my back on Mrs. Cummings and slowly walked to John's room.

October 1941

"Waronker did better this mornin'," Bill said approvingly. "He nearly got the whole thing right, save for that one sour note toward the end." Dan shook his head at Bill dismissively, and John just laughed.

I lifted my head up from my work and turned toward Bill. "What, Bill, you gotta assess the poor guy every mornin'?" I asked, wiping sweat from my brow. Bill frowned at me and continued to work.

"As long as you keep bitchin' about the fuckin' sand, then I can keep assessing him," he said firmly.

I scoffed but couldn't think of a decent comeback.

The hot sun bore down upon us as we cleared sand out of the bases of the guns. Fucking sand—always getting in places where it's not welcome and unwanted. The nerve of it. Our troop did a variety of different jobs a day. In the morning we maintained the coastal artillery guns, and then we'd move on to some of the preparation of the airstrip, and finally some training in the evening before we were dismissed. Some days it got pretty dull, but at least we weren't maintaining the trenches. I didn't want to imagine the horror of having to dig in the sand. As if I wasn't already covered in it. The sun progressed to being more overhead, and the heat became more oppressive. Even John had to take off his uniform shirt for comfort. Dan, Bill, Gary, and I had always taken ours off shortly after getting on site, not wanting the button-up shirt to get drenched in sweat, adding to our discomfort. Not John, he always toughed it out as long as he could because he was so conventional. Eventually the sun would get hot enough that even conventional John had to bow down to comfort.

"John, may I make an inquiry?" Gary eloquently asked one such afternoon. We were taking a break, drinking our canteens dry, and our sleeveless undershirts were stained with sweat and sand.

John just smiled at Gary's sweet innocence and nodded. "Sure, inquire away!" He chuckled deeply.

Gary smiled and took a swig from his canteen, water dribbling down his chin as he did so. He wiped his face on his elbow and pointed toward John's shoulder. "How'd you get that nasty scar on your shoulder there?" Gary's voice was innocent and curious, like a child's. John brought his canteen to his lips and paused, his eyes languidly moving over the rest of the guys to rest on me. I had been lying on my back with my arm over my eyes to shield the sun, but when Gary posed his question, I lowered my arm and turned toward John. John smiled at me; it was a somewhat cold smile that told me he was going to lie to Sweet Gary.

"Well that's actually an interesting story, Gary. Ben and I were—what, sixteen?—when it happened." John turned to me for support. I nodded and smiled at Gary, trying to go along with whatever tale John was about to expertly spin. John's face lit up with his magnificent plot and broke into a grin that didn't reach his eyes.

"Ben and I were always troublemakers growing up. One night we snuck out and hopped over to the neighboring town. When we got there, we decided to try and get some booze from the local bar, and we did pretty good. The bartender didn't even blink when we ordered drinks, and he kept them coming until we were good and hammered. Well Ben here is a dope; he was sloshed and was determined to pick up this one pair of legs." John cast a sideways look in my direction, laughing at the oncoming humiliation. I sniggered and shook my head, curious to see how my idiotic behavior had gotten him stabbed. Bill began to chuckle along with John, sensing that this was going to be a story he could use against me. Damn. Still chuckling, John carried on with his tale.

"So Ben swaggers over to this girl, beer in hand, and tries to pick her up. She's not having it and is trying to get rid of him, but Benny's so drunk he doesn't even notice. Well, I'm sitting at the other side of the bar, watching this horrible spectacle, when suddenly I see this huge guy." At this, John stood up and hunched his arms to illustrate just how large this behemoth of a man was. Gary's eyes got wide at the dramatics John was putting on and became completely enthralled with the story. Dan started laughing at John's antics, and I just watched, waiting to hear what kind of downfall I was about to take. John shot a quick look in my direction before returning to his theatrics.

"So this guy walks up to the pair of legs that wants nothing to do with Ben and wraps his arm around her. Now, had Ben been sober, he would've realized that this signaled the girl was taken, right?" John turned to his audience, engaging them as a great storyteller does. The guys nodded, falling into John's hypnotic trap of words. John smiled and slowly shook his head.

"Ben likes to blame it on the whiskey, but whatever the reason is—whiskey, obliviousness, or stubbornness—Ben doesn't let up." John gave a chuckle, and I had to laugh a little at that, and so did the other guys. It may have been a complete fabrication, but if it had happened, the truth probably wouldn't have been too far off, so I just kept my mouth shut and let John finish.

"Ben goes up to the guy and says, ''scuse me, sir, but I believe you're being awfully rude. The lady clearly doesn't want you near her.'" John shot a look in my direction and I scowled. All right, he lost his touch here. I would never have said such a thing! I would've told the ass bag that it was common courtesy to wait until the first suitor had left before attacking the poor woman. I shook my head and rolled onto my back again, replacing my arm over my eyes, no longer interested in the story.

"I'm guessin' the big guy didn't take too well to that, eh?" Dan asked helpfully, his grin full of teeth. John just chuckled and shook his head.

"Of course not!" said John. "So he shoves Ben, and Ben, of course, steps up to the fight even though he's drunk and can hardly stand, let alone throw a punch. The guy goes to hit Ben, and Ben just says something snarky back at him to piss him off even more. The guy hits Ben, and Ben goes sprawling on the bar. Of course Ben can't just leave it, so he starts pushing the guy's buttons and bein' a real jackass."

I nodded in agreement and casually continued to listen to the story. At least that part sounded like something I would've done. Actually, that sounded like something I'd done on several occasions—minus the alcohol.

"Eventually Ben hits a real nerve and I see the guy reach for a beer bottle." John paused here for dramatic effect. Gary gasped a little at this part, and it took all I had not to bust out laughing at the poor kid. John just took the sound as encouragement and pushed onward.

"He takes the bottle and he slams it over Ben's head, knocking him out. Then—I couldn't believe the nerve of the guy—he takes the broken bottle and goes to stab Ben even though he's unconscious and can't defend himself, all because Ben made some crack about fucking his mother!"

My eyes snapped open when John said those words, and I felt my body tense up. I tried to contain my reaction to his lie, but it was getting harder. I wished he would just wrap it up already.

Bill barked out a laugh and punched Dan in the shoulder. "Sounds like our Ben, all right!" I relaxed a little when Bill said that, and I relaxed even more when the rest of the guys laughed along with him. At least my idiotic sense of humor was good for something.

"This is a great story, but it still doesn't explain why you have a scar," Gary said, trying to get John to move along.

"True, I was getting there. So the guy's got the broken bottle and is going in to stab Ben, right?" The guys all nod in agreement, and their attentive behavior only fuels John. "I see this, and I leap across the bar—tripping over a couple of stupid drunkards along the way—and push Ben out of the way. But when I have my arms out and am pushing Ben out of the way, the guy brings the bottle down and catches my shoulder. Finally, the police show up and arrest the guy and drive Ben and me to the hospital, where we both got stitches. Ben's got a small scar on his head where the bottle was broken, and I have this one on my shoulder."

John turned to the side a bit so that they all got a good look at his scar. A small smile graced my lips at the whoas and oohs from the guys. John always got a kick out of making up a story that everyone bought. He said it was just like writing a story: simply fiction. I called it lying.

◆◆◆

John and I were lying quietly in our cots that night, just listening to the water as it sloshed up against the sandbar. I knew John was busy thinking, so I hadn't said much to him all night. As the waves continued to slosh, making me need to pee, I couldn't bear it any longer. I rolled onto my side and propped my head on my elbow, facing John. I could tell that John knew I was looking at him, but he didn't acknowledge that anything had changed.

"Do you ever intend to tell someone the truth about that scar?" I finally asked. I watched as John continued to lie on his back, staring at the canvas tent intently. He'd told countless lies about that scar, and I'd always gone along with them. In every fictitious account he'd created, he was always the hero saving someone— usually me. I never pressed him about it before, because I knew how much it killed him. That scar was a constant reminder of his defeat, and the first time that I had to save him.

"No," John finally whispered, letting that single syllable reverberate in the tent. I couldn't take my eyes off of him. I watched him intently, as though any movement he made might tell me what the hell he was thinking.

"What about Red? Will you ever tell her?" I asked, fearing what his answer might be. John remained still for a time, his chest just rising and falling with steady breaths. I watched for a couple more minutes until he turned on his side, facing away from me. That was the answer I was afraid of.

September 1935

John was lying on a bed of crisp white linen with a blanket draped over his legs. He was hooked up to several tubes that were pumping liquid into him, and his arm was wrapped in a sling across his chest. I took a couple of cautious steps into the room, not sure how I should proceed. John's eyes peeled open when he heard my boots on the tile, and he watched me steadily as I walked farther into the room.

"How ya doin', buddy?" I asked lamely. It was so strange to see him so damaged and helpless. This was not the valiant knight that I knew. Where was his shining armor? Where was his sword, his shield? I looked around the sterile white room and thought to myself, they're there, beaten up and broken on the chair. He wouldn't be using them anytime soon. John watched me in my discomfort, and the corners of his split lips turned up in a slight grin. The strange sight of John bandaged and smiling was hypnotizing, and I couldn't take my eyes off the creepiness of it.

"Next time you have a gun in your hands, Ben …" John said, his voice cracking. I stepped closer to the bed, held captivated by that eerie smile and those twinkling eyes. I nodded, urging him to finish.

"Don't miss."

October 1941

I watched John throughout the shift as he methodically did his job in silence. The other guys laughed and joked, and John occasionally joined in, but he told no more stories. After the previous night's admission, I began to count how many different lies John had spun about that single scar. There was the one he had told them the previous day, one where he fell on a broken glass bottle at the lake, one where he was saving some broad from getting mugged, and a few others like it where he was defending some girl's honor. All in all, I counted at least fourteen stories that I could recall; there were probably more that I'd never heard about that he told girls when he was lying next to them. I watched him closely, wondering if it ever bothered him.

"So why are we doing so much work on this airstrip? I mean, Pan Am's been here since thirty-five. Is it even meant to hold all our Wildcats?" Sweet Gary asked, changing the topic from humorous anecdotes to something more practical. I listened as Bill and Dan explained what we were really doing on this damn island. John swiftly replaced the piece he was cleaning and detached the next piece. The smoothness of his motions and the ease with which he did them told me that he had already forgotten about the scar lie and had brushed it off.

"Well, Gary," said Bill, continuing to work as he spoke. "Uncle Sam decided to put us Marines on Wake Island 'cause Pan Am had already constructed this airstrip. It shouldn't have any problem holdin' all our artillery and Wildcats."

"That's right," Dan said enthusiastically. "We here are ensurin' America's line of defense against the Japanese. If they take Guam, we're gonna be the closest airstrip to the mainland of Japan. In that scenario, all air strikes will come from our little island." His chest puffed out a little; he was clearly proud that we were all supporting the last line of defense. Gary nodded in understanding, his back straightening with Dan's contagious pride, and continued working.

"What if we're not ready when the enemy attacks?" Gary asked cautiously, a hint of fear tingeing his sweet voice and doubt curving his spine.

Bill let out a laugh and picked up another part to clean and reassemble. "Oh, don't ya worry, kid. We'll be ready for 'em."

I half-listened to their conversation while my frustration toward John began to mount. One more lie to add to his collection. He didn't even care. He should've cared.

"Yeah, but they could strike anytime!" Gary shouted worriedly.

Dan nodded and clapped a reassuring hand on Gary's small shoulder, stopping in his work to turn and address him. "Well sure, kid. It's a war! But it don't matter much when they hit us; I'll be damned if I let them fuckin' brutes get our island!"

Bill laughed in agreement and swung his thick arm across Gary's small shoulders. With a toothy grin, he said, "It'll be okay, kid. 'Sides, ain't it better ta go out a hero than a coward?"

Gary's frightened eyes looked to his other side, where Dan was standing, clearly hoping for something more comforting than the notion of an honorable death awaiting him. Dan shook his head at Bill and pushed his heavy arm off of Gary. Dan patted the kid's ginger head and simply shrugged, ending the discussion. John just smiled widely. I'd never understand how a man so concerned with being a noble gentleman, a true knight of honor, could be so comfortable with lying to the whole fucking world and carrying on as if it were nothing.

"What's up with youse?" Dan asked, throwing a strange look my direction, his face twisted in confusion and inquiry.

I shook my head and snorted again. "Nothin' man, just got some of this goddamn sand up my nose." Bill shook his head at me, Dan groaned, and Sweet Gary just laughed.

"Oh, you laugh now!" I shouted dramatically. "I said it once before! Just watch, it'll devour us all!" I waved my arms at the dreadful stuff and succeeded in making the rest of them cackle at my idiotic behavior. Gary threw a handful of sand in my direction and succeeded in covering my chest in the blasted stuff. I choked a little and tried to sweep the leeching grains from my torso. John shook his head at me, a light smile on his otherwise stoic features. I stared at him and tried to keep my smile sincere. That fucking sand might have been the bane of my pitiful existence, but John's lies were the chains of his honorable one.

"Devour us all," I whispered to myself, dropping my eyes to the work my hands were doing. John's smile slowly fell, and he didn't speak for the rest of the dreadful shift. Fucking lies.

◆ ◆ ◆

"That's a goddamn lie!" Bill shouted, thrusting his fork in Gary's general direction. Gary's eyes widened at Bill's forceful gesture. I looked up from my plate with a smile on my face at the current argument my team was having. I shook my head at Sweet Gary. After all this time with us, he was still green. Gary twitched away from the offending cutlery and looked into Bill's squinting eyes.

"I assure you, it's no lie," Gary replied, inching down the bench toward John and away from Bill's disbelieving glare. John snickered and continued to eat his dinner. Bill shook his head. I laughed and scooped some potatoes into my mouth.

"Why's it so hard to believe the kid, Bill?" Dan asked, patting Gary roughly on the back. Bill looked incredulously from Dan to Gary.

"Are ya fuckin' serious, Dan!" Bill shouted, gesturing at the kid with his fork and splattering some potatoes on my shirt. I rolled my eyes and picked off the lumps of white mush that landed on my chest.

"Yeah, Bill, I've gotta agree with Dan-o on this one. Why's it so hard to believe that the boy is engaged?" I asked, a smile pressed into my lips as I loaded up my fork with potatoes and flung it back at Bill. Bill glared at me and punched me in the arm.

"Don't throw your fuckin' food at me Benjamina!" said Bill.

"And unless ya want a nice concussion, I'd put that fork down if I was you."

I pouted and lowered my weapon, saddened that I couldn't lop the rest of my sand-filled dinner at the oaf. I pushed my tray away and leaned my elbow on the table.

"You still didn't answer the question Billy-boy! Why's it so hard to believe the kid's got himself a girl to marry?" John asked. I nodded in agreement and turned toward Bill, who had finally dropped his fork.

Bill scoffed at us. "Why? Because that kid is simply that! He's a boy, and all he's done is write the broad letters!" Bill spread out his large arms as if that were a sufficient answer. I looked over at Dan, who seemed just as confused as I was.

"So?" I said, not afraid to push the big guy's buttons. Sure, he could've laid me out flat in one punch, but he wouldn't have gone beyond knocking me unconscious. He respected me too much. Bill's mouth flapped open and closed for a minute in stunned silence, very much resembling one of the ugly fish we often saw along the shore.

"So? So how does his amateur poetry and lack of experience land him a girl!" Bill slammed his huge fist on the table, making his plate clatter with the disruption. I shook my head at Bill and glanced toward the other guys. Gary pouted a little at the insult and slumped on the bench. Dan rolled his eyes and thumped Gary supportively on the back. John simply remained silent and scooped another forkful of beans into his mouth.

"Yer okay, kid. Bill's just jealous that he don't got yer smarts to woo himself a pretty lady too," Dan said, snorting in amusement at his own insult. Gary and I laughed along with Dan, and even John chuckled at Bill's increasing frustration.

"I can get me any broad I want! And believe me, I have!" Bill said from behind clenched teeth as he pushed himself away from the table, nearly knocking it over on Dan, Gary, and John. Bill stomped away, and I watched his retreating back as he stormed off toward the barracks.

"Well, kid, I'm proud of ya. Congratulations!" Dan shouted, slamming his overly hairy hand on Gary's back once again. I saw the little ginger wince with each thump and knew Dan's "support" was quite painful for his small frame.

John laughed, distracting the Italian from his bruising congratulations. "Cool it, Dan. Try to be a little less excited. You'll dislodge one of the boy's organs before he can get married." I laughed and leaned back when John began to stack up our plates and trays to dispose of them. I pulled a toothpick out of my pocket and stuck it between my teeth to chew on.

"I do appreciate your support though, Dan. Thank you," said Gary.

John paused before picking up the trays and patted Gary's shoulder comfortingly, his eyes twinkling with genuine interest. "You'll have to tell us about her. What's this girl like that's had you weeping like a baby after each letter you write her?"

Gary's smile split his face, and he nodded enthusiastically up at John. If John hadn't been his Lancelot before, he sure as hell was now. I chewed on my toothpick a little harder and watched John as he strode over to the kitchens. Dan folded his arms in front of him on the table and leaned forward, putting the weight of his large chest on his hairy forearms.

"Benny," Dan whispered, catching my attention. I turned away from John's disappearing back and looked at Dan with large, innocent eyes.

"Oh, Danny boy; oh, Danny boy!" I sang, mirroring his position. Dan just frowned at me and gave a jerk of his head to signal that he was going to just ignore my stupidity.

"Yeah, anyway, what the fuck is up with Cummings? That's the most he's spoken all day!" Dan said in a harsh whisper, as if it were some huge, offensive secret. I rolled my eyes in an attempt to stall my response. The truth is I had been pondering the same thing all day, and I had no idea. All right, that's a lie. I had an idea. Maybe all those lies really did bother him. But most likely he just wanted to make sure he was not the center of attention for a while to avoid any more intrusive questions.

"Uh, John's just not a long-winded kind of guy," I replied, pursing my lips and nodding my head. Gotta sell this bullshit like it's gold. I guess it was the truth in a way, but I knew it wasn't what Dan was really asking about. Gary watched the two of us with wide, innocent eyes, as if he expected a secret to be divulged or something. Dan just stared at me like I was the biggest dumbass he'd ever seen. Which is probably true, but hey, I like to be in a league of my own.

"Bullshit," said Dan. "He may not speak often, but I've been on the receiving end of one of his speeches, and that boy is the definition of long-winded. Even so, he's been even less chatty today than usual, ya dumbass."

I nodded in agreement and looked over to the kitchens. I glanced back at Gary's eager eyes and knew I couldn't say that it was the kid's question that had shut John up. I opened my mouth to bullshit another answer when Bill—the big lug—decided to return.

"Mail came today," he said to us in his oh-so-eloquent way. I stared up at Bill as he dumped the browned and weathered envelopes on the table. Completely distracted by the letters and no longer concerned with John's elusive behavior, Gary leapt off of his bench and crawled across Dan to peek through the mail for a letter with his name printed on it. Dan leaned back to avoid being hit in the face with one of Gary's spastic elbows.

"Whoa, boy. Calm down!" Bill said as he flung his weight down on the bench beside me. Gary ignored Bill's comment and triumphantly grabbed his letters. He smiled boyishly at the two of them and returned to his seat beside Dan. "How come ya got two?" Bill asked, opening his own letter from his worried mother back in Nebraska.

Gary just smiled and held up his two letters with pride. "One's from Cindy, my girl. The other's from my mom—"

"Yer other girl. Got it, mama's boy," Bill said, opening his letter and reading it quietly to himself while his lips silently formed each word he read.

Gary shook his head and rolled his eyes. "You're more of a mama's boy than I am, Billy," Gary said, lowering his head to his own letters and ignoring Bill's glare.

I snorted at the two of them and continued to chew on my toothpick.

"There's one here for ya, Benny." Dan tossed the envelope toward me and grabbed his own. I looked down at the sender and recognized Mrs. Cummings's scrawled handwriting. I frowned and leaned over the table to try to locate John's letter. Mrs. Cummings never wrote me without writing John, too.

"Were these all of the letters for our section?" I asked when I noticed the only letters left on the table were the one from Gary's mother and one addressed to Dan.

Bill glanced up from his letter and nodded. "Yup," he said briskly before returning to his letter updating him on his Uncle Barry's mental condition, according to the words his lips mouthed noiselessly. I nodded and frowned at the letter in my hand before pulling the toothpick out of my mouth and tossing it on the ground.

"I'll catch up with you guys later." I stood up from my seat on the bench and began walking toward a thin spattering of trees by the shore. I wasn't about to read any letter from Mrs. Cummings in front of company, even if it was just the guys. Dan narrowed his eyes at me but nodded and let me go. I felt him watching me as I ripped open the envelope and pulled out the letter while I walked away. The sun was still out and warming my already perspiring skin when I finally sat down to read Mrs. Cummings's letter. And I found out exactly why she hadn't written John.

November 1940

I checked his eyes, hoping to see a fogginess of booze but there was none. They were crystal clear and I knew I was done for. I was happy to help the country, but the Marines? Serving, following orders, battle? This was more than a fistfight at a bar and I wasn't sure John knew that. I wanted to look my attacker in the eye, not have them rain down upon me without the possibility of a fair fight. I'd heard about the bombings over in London and that was the last fucking place I wanted to be. The country still needed men here, they needed men to tend the fields and harvest. They needed men at the mills to add the vitamins to the flour for our country so we didn't starve. That was noble enough for me.

"What about the mill?" I asked, hoping John would forget about this notion. Adventure was one thing, but honor and war was another.

John scrunched his face and shook his head. "What about it? Come on, I'll make an appointment with the recruiter. This is it, Ben. This is our chance to be heroes!"

His excitement washed over me and I cringed. I didn't want to be a hero. I wanted to just live my life—and I didn't care if I was called a coward or a chicken. But John did. John cared an awful lot. I had one final Hail Mary to get him to rethink it, but I knew he wasn't going to. We were as good as shipped off. "What about Red? I thought you said she was dropping out of college and moving here so you could get hitched?"

He didn't say anything for a while, but his blue eyes lost their spark and became sad as he looked down at his hands—his callused, browned hands sliding the pamphlets between his long fingers; those same hands that had just been touching her. I could tell from the way he kept touching his face while we were talking, discretely smelling her, committing it to memory.

"Yeah, well, plans change," he replied somberly. He wouldn't look up at me; I remember that.

"You break up?" I asked. I couldn't think of any other reason he'd willingly leave her. He just shook his head. I knew then what it was, but I wasn't going to say it.

"It's just time we had an adventure, don't you think?" He looked up at me, his eyes so hopeful and scared.

"You deserve her!" I wanted to tell him, but I knew he was too stubborn to listen. "This town's not so bad, you know; a decent place to raise a family. I can't think of anywhere better," I said, trying to be encouraging. We stared at each other for a while, his eyes still sad.

"We need something bigger; we're knights, after all," John said to me with a smile. It was a slight smile that turned up the corners of his lips and that was it. I nodded my agreement, and the spark immediately came back, although only half as bright. I looked at John and knew that he needed to feel the cold steel of a rifle in his hands before he felt those hands were worthy enough to touch a woman again.

October 1941

I lay on my cot after our long day in the sun, attempting to recover from the effects. Since the sun had slowly melted my brain and my mental stability was wavering from the damaging heat, I allowed myself to really wonder why I had agreed to join John on this adventure. I had nothing to prove, so why was I standing in the middle of hell every day holding a rag and mechanical parts filled with sand?

"John," I interrupted the quiet that had taken over our tent. I stared at the little holes in the canvas, my overheated brain finding familiar constellations in the punctures.

"Yeah?" he said, shuffling in his cot to turn toward me and, no doubt, arching his eyebrow imploringly. He always did that when he was preparing himself for something stupid to fly out of my mouth. He usually wasn't disappointed either.

"When we get back to Kansas, I'm never going back to the lake," I said. I stared unblinkingly at the canvas-tear constellations. I heard John shuffle in his bed a little and knew that his eyebrow had not been let down for its arching. What can I say? I wasn't one to disappoint.

"Why is that, Ben?" John asked with a chuckle, indulging my insanity brought on from the sun and exhaustion.

"Because once we get off this fucking island, I don't want to go near another grain of sand for at least twenty years." A gentle breeze shifted the canvas of the tent, and I lost my constellations. I heard the rumble of John's laughter and was immensely jealous; apparently the sun was not affecting his brain as it was mine. Damn him.

"All right, Ben, that sounds reasonable." He chuckled and rolled back onto his back, no longer facing me. As I lay there, the silence once again falling upon us, I couldn't stop another question from escaping from my lips. I knew it wasn't a smart question— hell, I knew I probably wouldn't get an answer considering all the other times I had asked it and received the same silent treatment— but I couldn't stop the words from freeing themselves of my lips.

"Have you written Red yet?" I asked. She was the whole reason my brain was oozing out of my ears right now and my current state. I didn't care if it was a touchy subject. John stiffened in the bed beside mine, and I waited patiently for him to speak. John just remained still, unmoving, unanswering, and pissing me off.

"Why do you feel you need to do this to be the man she deserves?" I asked. My voice was nearly a whisper, but I knew he heard it. If I was getting covered in layers of sand each night, risking the tiny granules slowly suffocating me in my sleep as I knew they were plotting to do, then I wanted a genuine answer.

"Why the fuck are we here?" I sat up, ignoring my precious canvas Perseus and his darling Andromeda to stare at a different hero. I had written in countless letters to Mrs. Cummings that John still loved Red, and she assured me that she had passed the message to Red in an attempt to make up for her idiot son not writing her. John didn't move, refusing to even acknowledge the conversation. John needed a push, and I was in the mood to shove him off a fucking cliff. I got off my cot and walked over to stand in front of him. If he wouldn't turn to me, I'd go to him. As much as he tried, he could never hide from me.

"What do you need to prove?" I asked. John stared up at me, his lips turning white from being pressed together so tightly, his jaw was set in a determined line, and his eyes were icy. I stared back; my brain was thinking clearer, but I wasn't about to back down.

"Drop it, Ben," he said, his voice a menacing rumble.

I shook my head and shoved my hand against his shoulder. It was rare for me to push John's buttons like this; the last time I did it was when we were twelve and I was trying to get him to report his Dragon to my pop. Eventually the Dragon took care of the whole mess by beating John to a pulp and leaving me no choice but to get my pop, anyway. However, the argument before all that happened resulted in my first broken nose. John had a hell of a right hook, and a temper to go along with it. I shoved John's shoulder again and knew from his eyes that he was reaching his breaking point; soon I'd be flat on my ass with another broken nose if I didn't watch myself.

"Why are we really here?" I asked, bending down to meet him eye-to-eye. I never said I was the sharpest tool in the shed, and I fully admit to not backing down when I should. John slowly sat up on his cot; his icy eyes stared unblinkingly at me. As I stared into those eyes, I finally saw it—the flash of red that was oh so familiar. The last time I had seen eyes like that, they were staring down a rifle barrel that was shaking in my hands.

I let out a dry chuckle. "At least write the girl and let her know you still love her and that this has nothing to do with her pretty ass!" I shouted into those raging eyes. I could see the punch coming from the pull of his shoulder, but for the sake of John's future happiness, I wasn't about to let him get out of this that easy. John swung his fist at me, and I ducked, forcing my body into his torso and tackling him off the bed. He pushed my shoulders back and rolled on top of me, slamming his fist into my left cheek. My head jerked to the side from the force, and I bit down on the inside of my cheek, drawing blood. I turned my head back to John, and my eyes were met with stormy eyes tinged with red.

"Your mom wrote and told me that Red doesn't believe her when she says you still love her. Your mom says Red's planning on staying in Maine; says there's nothing for her in Kansas and she's got another offer." I felt John tense, and his already heavy breathing picked up. I didn't mean to tell him so forwardly; in fact, I had no intention of telling him what the letter Mrs. Cummings wrote said at all. When I got pissed, though, all that kind of tactful thinking went out the window. I turned my head from him and spat out some blood on the fucking sand. I turned my head back toward John and stared boldly into the eyes of a Dragon.

"You're lying," John said, his thick fingers tightening into fists around my undershirt. I felt blood pooling in my mouth from my cheek, but I clenched my jaw tightly against his accusation.

"I'm not like you, John," I said, feeling his hold on my shirt grow tighter. I sat up into his clenched fists and stared into his eyes. "I don't lie."

I had barely gotten the last syllable out before John shoved my back against the sand and sent a fist into my gut. I jerked upward from the force of it and gasped. Blood trickled down my throat from the gasp, and I began to choke, sputtering blood on John's stony face and white undershirt. John refused to move and grabbed the straps of my sleeveless undershirt, pulling me toward him. He bent his head to stare into the truth of what I said and clenched his teeth.

"You're lying!"

He shook me a little. I smiled coldly at him and swung my left fist at his clenched jaw. John twisted from the force of my blow, and his grasp on my undershirt loosened. I twisted out of his fists and took a step back from him. I crouched down into a fighting stance, my fists in front of me, ready to take down this fucking knight.

"I told you, John. I'm not you. I don't fucking lie!" John lunged at me, and I swung my left fist into his right side before bringing my knee up into his gut. John doubled over and was taking in gasping breaths to refill his lungs. I took a step back and waited for John to regain himself.

"Just fucking write her and tell her the fucking truth!" I said, watching his back rise and fall with his heavy breaths. John looked up at me, the red very prominent in the stormy gray, and I knew the Dragon was about to attack. John growled and charged me, toppling me backward and slamming me onto the deceivingly hard sand. "Fuck-ing sa-nd," I said, gasping out.

John lifted his head and clamped both of his large, rough hands on either side of my face. "Prove it to me," he said.

My eyes widened slightly in surprise at the demand, and I quickly tried to cover it up. John slammed my head against the sand and then lifted it back toward his face.

"Show me!" he shouted, spittle flying out of his mouth and getting in my eyes.

I blinked involuntarily, and my eyes began to tear from the invasion. I tried to shake him off of me, but John was solid.

"Show it to me!" he shouted again.

I heard sloshing in the sand and shouting from a distance. I just stared into John's twisted face and glared silently. "Maybe you really are just like him," I whispered. I felt John's hurt and surprise at my comment more than I saw it. His body tensed, and his hands began to slide off my face before they were gone entirely. I watched as Bill lifted John off of me and restrained him. Dan stood between the two of us, staring at John, almost daring him to try to break free from Bill's grasp. Gary slowly lifted me up from the sand, and we all stared at John.

"Show me," he said again softly. I wanted to shake my head at his stupid stubbornness, but the swelling in my cheek and the pounding in my head prevented me from doing so. Dan moved aside and turned slightly to look at me curiously. I ignored all of their questioning stares and just scoffed at John.

"Why the fuck would I show a Dragon?" I turned and spit out more blood, watching it splatter on the ground by Gary's bare feet. John lunged at me, and Bill tightened his hold on him. I glared at him and stumbled out of the tent with Gary's help. I followed Gary to his tent across the way from ours silently. When we got to Gary's tent, he showed me to the currently empty cot beside the one he obviously was sleeping in and watched me collapse upon it.

"What the flying hell was that all about?" he asked, taking a step back from my crumpled form and running his fingers through his red hair in distress. I just stared straight ahead and didn't move; every muscle in my body was screaming and on fire.

"It's not about her," I said. Gary stared at me, perplexed. "It's about him."

November 1940

"Are you sure you want to do this?" I asked him cautiously. I already knew the answer given the steely look in his eyes and the thin line his lips were pressed into that only slightly let the bitter smell of alcohol escape. John gave me a terse nod and lifted his chin defiantly. He squared his shoulders and lifted his chest, just the way I knew he had always envisioned; the only things missing from his battle-ready stance were the chainmail and shiny armor. The porch light flickered a little as John slowly climbed the wooden stairs to the Dragon's lair.

I watched silently from the bottom of the stairs, where I always watched, the damp grass crushing beneath my feet, the blades bending to accommodate the oppressive weight of my shoes. I watched silently as John slowly raised his rough hand to the door handle. John paused, his hand on the handle his fingers had gripped since he was an infant, hesitating as if he had never touched it before, had never felt its metal before, as if the grooves and chipping paint were all new sensations to be felt. I zipped up my canvas jacket and shoved my hands in my pockets, my eyes never leaving his tall figure.

While John stood at the door, frozen, I could hear some stomping coming from inside the house. Soon there was faint yelling, muffled by the structure of the house, and then all was silent and the movement ceased. John removed his hand from the door handle and stuffed it into his jacket pocket. He shook his head as if he were awakening from a daze, as if he were confused, as if he had failed. I stood in the damp grass and watched as he abruptly turned from the door and climbed down the wooden steps that lead to the Dragon's lair. His armor slowly fell off of him and clamored unglamorously to the ground with each heavy step he took toward me. His eyes were downcast, and he refused to glance at me when he stopped at my side. I simply nodded and turned to walk beside him as we trudged our way from the Dragon's dwelling.

John stared quietly at his shoes, contemplating each foot as it was placed in front of the other. I raised my head to look at the stars. The night air was crisp and cool, but the sky was clear and the stars sparkled like tiny swords. I began counting constellations and recalling their mythos. Andromeda, named for the princess that was tied to a rock to be a sacrifice for a sea monster but was rescued by Perseus. Perseus, who stood by Andromeda, poised to always protect her. Orion, the hunter accidently killed but so beloved by Artemis that he was put into the sky. I glanced down at John, who solemnly lifted his head toward the twinkling gazes of the November stars. He blinked at them for a time before lowering his head once more in shame, knowing that the heroes in the sky had witnessed his cowardice.

One day that Dragon would be slain; until then, I simply walked beside John in mutual silence of understanding and acceptance.

November 1941

We sat uncomfortably at breakfast the next morning. Bill had stayed with John the night before to calm him down and make sure he wouldn't come after and kill me. I knew he wouldn't; he was angry but not homicidal. I glanced up from my plate and saw his piercing eyes, which were still staring at me coldly. Maybe he was a little homicidal after all. I continued eating slowly while the others attempted to regain conversation as normal. Gary had tried again that morning to pry into what had caused John to lose his thick layer of calm and attack me, but I just shrugged and got dressed in some borrowed pants and a clean shirt. How could I tell Sweet Gary that I had pushed a couple of buttons and let out the dormant dragon within his precious Lancelot? Answer: I couldn't. Dan kept looking at me from under his thick, bushy, frowning eyebrows. He kept quiet, but I knew he was working on a way to get me alone so he could figure out what had happened. I knew he had seen the name of the sender on the letter he handed me at dinner the previous day, and since his questioning about John's silence, he had only gotten more curious.

"I heard we had ourselves a little dispute last night. Is that true, privates?" Captain Michaels said demandingly from behind us in a booming voice. I winced a little and sucked on my swollen lip. Gary had told me that my cheek looked like a plum that had sprouted from my teeth; the blue-and-purple coloration covered that entire side of my face. I looked at John and noticed that he had similar coloration on his cheek, only without so much swelling.

Dan tried to cover for us, standing up to address Captain Michaels respectfully. "Uh … yes, sir … there was … uh … an incident last night."

Captain Michaels looked at John, who lowered his stormy eyes, and then rested his steely gaze upon me. "Halpert, you will have kitchen duty for the rest of the week. Dishes and cleanup!"

I nodded silently and looked over to John, who had raised his eyes to proudly meet the Captain's punishment for him.

"Cummings, you will be temporarily placed with Connor's section in the trenches."

John nodded stiffly. I tried to hide the frown that covered my face. Of course John would just get reassigned and not an actual punishment; Captain Michaels wants to suck his dick too much. I rolled my eyes and looked back down at the wooden table. Captain Michaels turned to the rest of our section and narrowed his eyes contemplatively at them. He took in a deep breath through his long, straight nose and blew it out just as roughly.

"The rest of you—"

"Sir," said Dan, cutting the captain off, "I'd like to volunteer to do kitchen duty with Halpert today." We all stared at Dan with confusion. I tilted my head to the side and gave him a look like he was insane. I knew he wanted to talk, but only an insane person or a masochist would really volunteer to do kitchen duty. It was bad enough to be out in the sun all day, but sitting in a humid, partially covered makeshift kitchen with little to no airflow was pure death.

Captain Michaels regarded Dan curiously before giving a curt nod of his head and agreeing. "Very well, private." He then turned to Bill and Gary and pointed at them. "You two." He paused and briefly considered the two contradicting body types before him and shook his head. "You two will be on guard duty on the eastern perimeter." Gary gulped, and Bill gave an accepting nod. Captain Michaels swept a calculating look over our section and nodded. "Get to it. Any more 'incidents' and your punishments will far outweigh the pain you're in today." The Captain turned to John and me at that last part and addressed us both. We nodded silently in understanding, and the Captain spun around and left us. I let out a long sigh and resumed my seat, running my fingers through my hair in exasperation. Our section sat there in silence for a while, picking at the remaining food on our plates. Even Bill and Gary were unsure of how to proceed with conversation.

"I hear you'll be joining my section for the day, Cummings," Jim said, interrupting our very uncomfortable silence. I looked up at Jim and snorted. He turned his eyes briefly to me before going back to John. John looked briefly up at Jim and nodded. "Well, we are heading out. Finish up, pretty boy, and let's get to work!" Jim said, his back straightening—no doubt from the stick lodged up his ass. John nodded again and stood up from the bench with his tray in his hand, preparing to take it back to the kitchens. John paused once he was standing up and glared coldly back down at me. He let his tray slip through his loosening fingers and clamor on the table. I stared up at him unflinchingly.

"Cummings, let's go!" Jim said again.

I tilted my head at Jim and gave John a tense smile. "Yup, you'd best be off, Cummings. Don't worry; I'll take care of your tray today." I grabbed his overturned plate and stacked it on top of mine. John snarled at me and leaned forward so his face was in mine.

"Cummings!" Jim shouted again, pulling on John's shoulder. John just shrugged him off and ignored his forceful prodding.

"All you had to do was show me the goddamn letter," he hissed his words in my face.

I just stared up at him, into his stormy, angry eyes. I watched out of my peripheral vision as Jim stopped his attempts to pull John away and stared at me with a slight tilt to his thin lips. I wasn't sure what Jim meant behind that smirk, but I ignored it and continued to stare into John's eyes.

"I don't have it anymore," I replied simply. I saw John's body tense and Jim's smirk grow.

John took a deep, shaky breath and pulled away from me. He nodded at Jim and gestured for him to lead the way. Jim smiled at me before turning around and leading John to his section.

I watched as the men retreated toward the trenches, my body becoming stiffer with each step they took.

"What's up with youse?" Dan said, stacking up all of our table's trays to carry back to the kitchen. I shook my head and turned back to help him.

"Nothin'," I replied, heading toward my temporary doom.

May 1941

"So you're really going?" Mrs. Cummings asked, her head lying on my chest with her sunny blonde locks fanned out against my skin. I nodded, my fingers entwining in her feathery soft hair and pulling gently so the yellow strands ran through my fingers. Her delicate hand was tracing circles along my stomach while she processed my answer. We finally got our date to start the twelve weeks of our Marine Corps Recruit Training and we were due to ship out for it in three days. She slowly sat up and turned to look into my eyes. "Promise me that you'll look out for him."

I looked into her clear blue eyes and couldn't stifle the laugh that came to my lips. "You want me to look out for him?" I laughed harder at the notion.

Her body rose where she was leaning on me from the chuckles coming from my chest. She narrowed her eyes at me and slapped my chest. "Benjamin! I mean it!"

I stopped laughing and stared into her serious face as I shook my head and frowned.

"He's being foolish; you and I both know it. He's not doing this for any kind of 'honor' for the country." Her clear eyes bore into mine, begging me to listen to her.

"How can I look out for him when he's the one that's always saving my ass?" I asked, propping myself up against the pillows behind me. Mrs. Cummings just laughed; it was a gentle laugh that sounded like bells.

"Not always, Ben," she said. She rolled off of me and began looking for her clothes. I watched as she slid her hose up her legs and zipped up her skirt. She didn't say anything more until she was fully dressed with her white blouse tucked into her gray skirt and her red pumps slipped on her feet. She walked to my bedroom door and paused, the moonlight washing out her features in its ghostly glow. She turned back to me where I was still lying in my bed, unmoving. "Just don't let him ruin the life he has here while he's seeking his glory or whatever over there."

I nodded and watched as she silently snuck out of my house and walked back toward her husband, the Dragon.

November 1941

I ran the back of my hand against my brow, collecting the beads of sweat that were forming there again. I let out a heavy sigh and continued scrubbing the stack of dishes before me. I heard Dan plunge a pot into the tub of soapy water and begin to scrub. We had been working in silence for the past two hours and seventeen minutes. Not that I was counting. Yeah, okay, I totally was. What else was I supposed to do? I knew Dan had every intention to talk to me about John and the current condition of my face, but until he brought it up, I was just going to keep counting the seconds until the noon meal. I dunked the plate I had just scrubbed into the tub of rinsing water beside me and washed off all the suds.

"How long have you and John been friends?" Dan asked, startling me from my silent counting.

I paused in my dunking and furrowed my brow in concentration. One, that was not the question I thought he was going to ask; and two, I had to really think about my answer. I met John when we were seven; we were twenty-two at the time. "Uh, fifteen years or so," I said. I kept my head down and began scrubbing the next dish. There was one good thing about all the sand: it made it easier to scrub all the dried food particles off of the plates.

"Have ya ever gotten in a brawl like last night before?" Dan asked. I narrowed my eyes and glanced at him out of the corner of my eye. I wasn't entirely sure where he was going with this very fact-based interrogation.

"We've had our fights. Nothin' quite like that, no," I said.

Dan dunked the pot into the rinsing tub and reached for the next one in his queue. It was unexpected for Dan to volunteer to do this labor with me. I mean, we had never been what you would call "close." He was in my section, and sure, we joked around, but nothing more. We never had heartfelt conversations, and until John told the lie—I mean story—about his scar, he never showed any interest in me or my life. I watched him scrub the pot, the black hair on his forearms getting matted down against his tan, olive-colored skin.

"Have I ever told ya 'bout how me and Bill met?" Dan asked. I dropped the plate I was scrubbing in the soapy water and turned to look at Dan. Confusion was creasing my face, and I was lost, having no idea where this conversation was really going.

"Uh, no, ya haven't," I said apprehensively. Dan kept scrubbing his pot, making sure to get into every nook and cranny. Clearly this was not his first time in the kitchen; Dan was a dish master! As I watched him scrub, I began picturing Dan in a New Jersey diner, wearing a stained white apron and yelling in a thick Jersey accent about a cannoli or some shit like that.

"We met in the Marines; that much ya already knew."

I nodded in agreement and turned back to my dishes. I knew Captain Michaels would have my head if he saw me just watching Dan work, even if it was because the guy wasn't making any sense.

"What ya don't know is that three years ago, when I met Bill, I had enlisted in the Marines with my little brother."

I furrowed my brow. I had no idea Dan had a little brother; he had never mentioned him before. I kept washing, now paying much more attention to what Dan was saying. I wasn't sure how this related to me and John, but I could tell that Dan had a point he was making and that he was going to make it big.

"He was only nineteen when we enlisted, but he was so excited. Gary reminds me of him sometimes. He wasn't quite as green as Gary is, but he was just as youthful and energetic." Dan let out a strained laugh, his head hanging low over the pot in his hands. "Anyway, joining was my idea, but Gabe went everywhere I did. Gabe had been taggin' along with me since we were kids. When we got to Oahu, it was a whole different world from Jersey. Gabe was so excited to be in a tropical place like that. He was originally bunked with Bill, while I was bunked with some guy named Nick. Bill was—well, is—a brute, and he gave Gabe a lot of shit. Bein' the big brother, I never let no one pick on my lil' bro. Naturally, Bill and I didn't get along for those first couple of months he was roomin' with Gabe."

I frowned and dunked my plate in the rinsing tub. "I'm confused; you guys hated each other when ya first met?" I asked.

Dan flashed a smile, all of his white teeth showing as it stretched across his face. "Yup, we sure did."

I nodded my head, encouraging him to continue.

"I know Bill was just tryin' to toughen Gabe up, same as we're doin' with Gary now. But when it's yer little brother that you've been takin' care of since ya were three, well, ya don't look down at those actions quite so friendly. Gabe took it all in stride; he was very patient and wanted to prove himself. He never had any problems with Bill; said he was a stand-up guy, actually. Gabe would tell me to relax, that Bill was just a little dense but an overall good guy. I didn't want to listen, 'cause let's face it, my little brother couldn't know better than me." Dan started chuckling at his jab to himself. I laughed a little with him, unsure if I should have been laughing or not. It was one of those awkward moments when you don't know what reaction you're supposed to have since you don't know where it's going.

"Well, one night at dinner Bill was layin' into Gabe, and it was pissin' me off. Gabe just sat there smilin', laughin' at the shit Bill was sayin'. Well, I just lost it. I couldn't believe that Gabe would let a guy talk to him like that. I swung at Bill and hit the big lug square in the jaw! Well, you can't just hit a guy like Bill and expect that to be it. Bill swung back at me, and the next thing I know we're in a huge brawl in front of everyone. Gabe eventually pulled me off of him and took a swing at me! My little bro had never hit me before, and it shocked the sense right outta me. Next thing I knew, Gabe and I were fightin'. He was picking his punches good just like I taught him." Dan smiled sadly into his pot and paused in his scrubbing. He turned to me then, dropping the pot in the sudsy water. "Do ya know what happened next?" he asked.

I shook my head, turning my back to my dishes and watching him.

Dan looked down at his hands, which were dripping with water, before looking back at my face. His eyes had a fire in them that I hadn't seen before, considering he was typically such a laid-back guy. "There was some yellin', we both said some stuff you should never say to a person ya love, and then we parted ways. We didn't talk again for the next two days. We were both stubborn assholes; even Bill couldn't get us to come together." Dan let out a dry laugh but kept staring at me as if looking away might make me miss his point.

"Bill even went so far as to seek me out durin' duties and tell me that I needed to go talk to my brother. I just ignored him, 'cause again, how could he know better than me?"

"So you and your brother haven't spoken since?" I asked hesitantly. I was trying to build a connection between Dan's story and what was going on between me and John, but I was struggling. I guess John and I were practically brothers, and if I never spoke to him again I'd wind up with Bill as my best friend? I wondered if that was what Dan was saying.

Dan jerked his head slightly to the side, his square jaw tensing. "My brother is dead." His voice was hoarse and practically growling at me, but his volume was quiet. I shut my mouth immediately and knew that this was one time I absolutely shouldn't speak.

"We never spoke again because two days after our fight, Gabe was loadin' up a battleship with some supplies and a couple of crates filled with artillery fell on top of him. Gabe was crushed to death under the weight. Some dipshit stacked the boxes wrong and killed my little brother," Dan said, his volume getting softer but his tone maintaining its firmness. He took a step toward me, his wet hands dripping soapy water on the sand-covered ground beneath our boots.

"Don't let some petty shit and stubbornness prevent you from bein' a man and ownin' up to a mistake. You don't need to face battle to lose someone out here. Accidents happen, too."

I lowered my eyes, unable to stare into his even if they were filled with a wisdom I knew I should listen to. Dan turned back to his work and left me staring at my boots in the muddy dirt by the tubs of water.

"John's mom sent me a letter tellin' me that his girl is gonna move on because he's being a dumbass and ignoring her," I said to Dan.

Dan kept washing his pots, but I knew he was listening. "Is that what the fight was about?" he asked. I shook my head and turned back to my dishes. I marveled at how wrinkly and slimy my hands felt after being submerged in the water for so long. I thrust them back into the tub and began to scrub another plate.

"Kinda. I pushed his buttons last night so that he wouldn't let her slip through his fingers 'cause he doesn't think he's good enough for her." Dan snorted at the notion but didn't say anything.

"I thought we came here because of her, but really we came here because of him," I said as I plunged another plate into the rinsing tub and grabbed the next one beside me.

"Him?" Dan asked, confused.

I didn't reply, not willing to divulge that kind of information.

Dan nodded at my silence and didn't press any more down that road. "Is that the letter John was talkin' about this mornin'?" Dan asked instead.

I let out a sigh and nodded. "Yeah."

"Then why don't youse just show it to him? Let him read it for himself. What's the big deal?" Dan asked. His pile of pots was actually growing smaller, and I couldn't figure out for the life of me how he was doing it. He really was a dish master.

I shook my head and put another clean plate aside. "I can't," I answered.

Dan threw the pot he was washing into the tub and stormed over to me. He pushed my shoulder back so I was facing him instead of the tub. He shoved his square jaw and dark eyes into my face and stared me down. "You're tellin' me that you're gonna let a fuckin' letter ruin yer friendship?"

I flinched and shook my head. "If it was just a letter, I would let him read it," I said quietly. No matter how close you are to someone, "I'm in love with your mom" is never easy to say. I watched as Dan's brows furrowed together, the bushiness of them creating a shadow over his eyes.

"Whaddya mean?" he asked, not backing down from his proximity to me.

I swallowed and tried to look away, but he was so close that I couldn't. "Well, Mrs. Cummings and I have a bit of a secret that John doesn't know about," I said apprehensively.

Dan's frown deepened, and he took a step back, giving me some air to breathe. "And that is?" he asked tentatively.

I swallowed and ground the heel of my boot in the mud. "That I've been in, uh … in an 'affectionate relationship' with her for, ya know, a couple of … years." I glanced up to watch Dan's expression turn into one of complete shock and criticism. Shame filled me instantly and I bowed my head farther down to keep scrubbing.

"Don't show him that letter," he finally said, after he regained his sense.

I pursed my lips and nodded. "Yup," I replied, and I turned back to my dishes. Well, that was helpful.

◆ ◆ ◆

Dan and I stayed in the kitchens through dinner—eating beside the tubs of water that we had to empty and refill twice—until finally every last dish was clean and all the equipment had been set aside for us to do it all over again the following day. Fun. At least we had the rest of the evening to relax. Even though everyone was kept busy until the last possible hour, we could usually squeeze in an hour or so to unwind before we retired for the night. Dan and I walked over to our typical table in silence. Neither of us had brought up the subject of John again after I told Dan my secret about Mrs. Cummings. We didn't know what more to say, I guess. His disapproval was obvious—and expected—but what was unexpected, was that he didn't seem to despise me for it. I knew how wrong it was for a man to do to his friend what I did; I deserved for him to condemn me, or at the very least detest my guts. I glanced over at Dan in the silence to gauge his level of resentment, but he was relaxed and unbothered by my company. At least I could catch some kind of break with him, it seemed. Maybe I could somehow be just as lucky with the others, too.

After about thirty minutes, Bill and Gary finally joined us. They were joking about their guard duty and how useless Gary was. Dan and I smiled and listened to their banter, happy for a distraction from our awkward silence. After hearing Dan's story about his brother earlier, I started paying closer attention to Bill's interaction with Gary. He was picking on him, to be sure, but from Dan's description, Bill was a lot easier on him than he had been on Gabe. I watched the three of them and recognized the protectiveness that the two older men had for Sweet Gary.

"Who's up for a game of cards?" Bill suddenly asked, disturbing me from my observations. I nodded, and the smile on Gary's face made it look like he'd never been invited to play cards before.

"Sure, I got my deck in my foot locker; I'll go get it," Dan said, and he jumped up from the table. I watched Gary, who was bouncing slightly with excitement, as Bill turned to him.

"Do ya know how to play five-card poker, boy?" Bill asked. Gary nodded and began rattling off the rules and what hand trumped what. I stared at him in shock, considering the way he was explaining the game. He was so technical about it! I swear that school had drilled the fun out of every subject for him. I groaned and put my hand up to stop him midlist.

"Whoa, kid. Clearly ya know the game, but shit, have ya ever played it?" I asked. I saw Gary kind of stop bouncing and run his thin fingers through his red hair. He dropped his eyes to the table and shrugged before shaking his head.

"Nah. I learned the rules because I always wanted to play, but none of the other boys were interested. Well, at least not enough of the boys at school were interested."

I nodded and accepted his answer. "Well, you're in for a treat tonight then," I said, and his smile returned with more enthusiasm. Dan returned with his deck and began shuffling the worn and slightly dirt-covered cards.

"Just do me a favor, kid," I said, gaining Gary's full attention and effectively calming his excitement. I leaned forward onto the table a little and stared into his twinkling eyes. "Just leave the technicalities out of it and enjoy the fuckin' game." I smiled at him and leaned back. Gary nodded at me, his bouncing excitement gone but his lips still curved up in a smile.

Bill clapped him on the shoulder and pounded his back a couple of times while Dan began to deal. "And don't forget yer poker face, boy!" he said with a chuckle.

I smiled at the advice and watched as Gary's smile quickly turned into an exaggerated scowl. I let out a laugh at the ridiculousness of his poker face. His forehead creased in lines that I was sure it had never seen before, and his lips struggled to stay downturned and kept twitching involuntarily at the corners. I looked over at Bill, whose eyebrows were creasing tightly together in an attempt to pull his own smile back.

Dan finished dealing and just chuckled. "Calm down, Gary. Youse don't have to scowl like that the whole game! Hell, Benjamina here smiles the whole fuckin' time, and Bill nods when he gets a card he likes." Dan pointed at each of us as he addressed us.

I started laughing harder when Bill glared at Dan. "I do not!" he protested childishly.

I punched Bill in the shoulder lightly. "Yeah ya do, buddy. Ya also shake your head when ya get a card that just messed up your hand!"

Bill turned his glare to me and punched me back. I winced a little at the force, considering I was still quite bruised and sore from my brawl with John, but I quickly covered it up with a smile.

"All right, all right, settle down," said Dan. "Gary, relax yer poker face; Ben, stop laughin'; and Bill, just accept yer tells and stop glarin' at Ben."

Bill gave me one last glare and turned to his cards, following orders. I let out one more chuckle before taking a deep breath and picking up my cards. I looked across the table from me at Sweet Gary and noticed that his face was much more natural and that his brow was now creased in familiar lines of concentration as he studied his cards.

I studied my cards and slammed two on the table and slid them toward Dan on my right. "Two."

Dan dealt me two cards and placed my other ones on the burn pile. I watched Bill gently shake his head and select three cards to exchange. I smiled and watched as each player exchanged cards and showed his tells. My smiled broadened when my turn came around again, and I exchanged one card. I was absolutely going to lose.

◆ ◆ ◆

We played three games before John showed up, and thank God we weren't playing for any money. The sun had set long before, and the camp was lit by a couple of hanging lights around the dining area, but only for another hour or so, and then we had to turn in.

Gary had won two of the games, and Dan had won one. I was getting my ass kicked, but that was okay; it was all in good fun, and I wasn't actually losing anything, which made it pleasant. We were on our fourth hand when John came walking up. I briefly glanced up at him before slapping two cards down to exchange.

He was walking slowly, and he was carrying something in his left hand. I watched as he trudged his way into the lights of the dining area. His face was stoic, completely void of all emotion, but his eyes were burning as the dragon I had glimpsed last night made his way to my table. Gary exchanged one card and Dan studied his hand intently.

I glanced around the dining area, evaluating which sections were sitting in there and which ones weren't. Unfortunately, Jim's section had been sitting in the far right corner adjacent from me since dinner. Jim had been a late arrival, rejoining his group about an hour after they had claimed their table. I didn't think anything of it at the time, figuring he had stayed back with John to put away the tools and set up for tomorrow. I was familiar with the process. When John didn't show up with him, I figured it was because he was still batshit angry with me.

"Ben, what's yer play?" Dan asked, trying to get my attention back on the game.

Considering the way John was walking toward me, navigating his way through the tables without taking his fiery eyes off of me, made me realize that 'batshit angry' was now an understatement. His shoulders were pulled back tightly, pushing his chest outward, and his back was rigid. He was marching into battle, his shield on his back and his sword at his side, ready to cut down his opponent with one swing.

Dan lowered his cards and followed my gaze, watching John make his way to us. I saw the muscles in Dan's arms flex and knew that he understood John's body language, too. Gary looked at the two of us in confusion, and Bill just took in a deep breath and slowly let it out.

August 1929

"Where ya goin', John?" I asked breathlessly as I ran after him, my tiny legs shaking under the force of my adrenaline. John was walking deceivingly fast several yards in front of me. I winced at the pounding in my head and knew that the cut at the corner of my right eyebrow was bleeding again as a slimy substance dripped down my face.

He addressed me without turning or halting his steps. "They beat you up," he said simply. He continued forward, determination in every step his small frame took. I finally caught up with him and grabbed his arm. I was panting heavily from my run and squatted to catch my breath beneath my bruised ribs. I shook my head in an attempt to clear it, and John just waited patiently. I had been waiting for John to walk home from school when a younger boy came running up and told me that John was going to confront the junior high boys that beat me up. I didn't hesitate to catch up to him.

"I know they did, John. I was being stupid and talking big with a couple of seventh graders," I said, gasping for air while still holding onto his arm. John nodded and took a step forward to continue his march. I tightened my grip on his arm and stopped him from proceeding while I caught my breath.

"So what, John? It's okay; it's not the first time, and you know it."

John nodded in agreement and turned to face me, briefly giving up on his quest. "You really do need to learn to shut your mouth," he said.

I shrugged my small shoulders and nodded. "Yeah, but where's the fun in that?" I said, a smile covering my face and pulling at the tender skin around my black eye. John just stared coldly at me, his arms down at his sides, unmoving. My smiled faded, and I stared back at him. "Just let it go, John. They're two years older than us, and you'll be outnumbered! Do you really think that just one twelve-year-old could do this to me?" I asked, pointing to my cut eyebrow and swelling black eye. I lifted up my striped shirt and showed him the bruising on my ribs from where the older kid's friends had thought it was funny to kick me.

John's face remained emotionless as he looked over my wounds, but his eyes began to blaze. He raised his flaming eyes to mine, and that was the first time I ever saw a glimpse of the dragon that lay within them. "It's not honorable, Ben. They deserve to be shown what true honor is," John replied coldly.

I stared at him, my mouth agape in surprise. "Honor?" I said, my grip loosening from his wrist. John smiled and pulled his arm away from me. He began trudging again toward the junior high school a mile away.

"Honor, Ben. Just like real knights!" he said. And with those words, I watched him walk determinedly into battle.

November 1941

I'd seen John walk into numerous battles with the same stance he was walking toward me with. After that first fight, when we were ten, I always walked proudly behind him just like a good squire would. But now, as we all watched John approach our table and halt just behind Sweet Gary, I was the one he was marching toward. I took in a shallow breath and waited for him to draw his sword and proclaim a duel, just as I'd witnessed a hundred times before. We stared at each other for a couple of minutes; no one made a single move except to draw in and release breath. I heard shuffling behind us and knew that Jim's section was watching intently. The entire dining hall around us seemed to fade away and freeze in time, as if they had never existed. John slowly raised his left hand and let the bundle that he was carrying fall onto the wooden table with a loud, resounding thud.

I continued to stare into his blazing eyes, refusing to look at the item on the table. I heard Dan take a sharp breath to my right, and I saw him start to shake his head in my peripheral vision. John took in a long, deep breath through his nose and let it out with equal harshness.

"Why has my mother been writing to you, Ben?" John asked coldly.

I glanced down at the stack of letters I had kept wrapped in my underwear in my footlocker. I guess my security device couldn't keep him out. I remained silent and waited.

John slowly reached out and grabbed the letter on the top of the stack. He eased it delicately out from under the twine that held them all together and lifted it up. Mrs. Cummings's scrawled handwriting flashed at me ominously, guiltily, seductively.

"I was informed earlier today that you had a stack of letters that you kept with you, and that the addressee was an unusual person. Thinking to myself that it was impossible that you'd lie to me about something like that, I went looking through your footlocker once I got off duty. At first everything seemed in order—well, in order for you anyway—until I noticed a pair of your underwear wedged in the far back corner of the locker," John said. He tilted the letter toward him and studied the handwriting and the address. The fire in his eyes briefly disappeared to reveal the immense sadness that was coursing through him. He turned the letter over and over in his hands and watched the browned paper slide over his fingers. After a time, he brought his eyes back to me, the sadness once again replaced by rage.

"I remembered that when we were little you used to hide your favorite toys that way, thinking that no one would dare touch your underwear and thus would never look there." He let out a very dry chuckle and turned the letter in his hands again. "Imagine my surprise when I unwrapped your underwear to find this stack of letters. I thought they were simply from your family—your mom begging you to come home safely, as I know she does. But no, not a single letter was from your family; not a single letter in this entire stack was from your mom. They are all from mine." He growled out the last word and threw the letter in his hands forcefully in my face.

There it is, the gauntlet was cast and the duel proposed, I thought, closing my eyes when the worn corners slapped my face and fell back to the table. I opened my eyes and slowly stood up from my bench. John watched me, his jaw clenching threateningly, and I knew that he was about to unsheathe his sword and take a swing at me.

"How long have you been fucking my mother?" he asked menacingly. His voice was low, rumbling, and dripping with snarling venom. I stared at him as I felt John's sword go through my stomach in a searing flash of pain.

Bill reached out a large hand and wrapped it around Gary's shoulder. Bill scooted backward on the bench and slowly pulled

Sweet Gary with him, removing him from the line of fire. For once in my life, I didn't say anything; I just gazed into the fiery eyes that were burning through me.

John's lips pulled back in a snarl, and he slammed his fist on the table with a force that caused the stack of letters to fall over. Dan slowly stood up and hunched forward, ready to grab either of us to prevent a fight. I set my jaw and took in a deep breath.

"How long?" John said with a growl, his volume rising.

I could feel Jim and his men watching us, and I knew that they were not the only ones. Usually I didn't think before getting into a fight; usually I didn't stop talking shit long enough to process anything beyond the current situation. But with John, with this fight, I couldn't allow this to get out of control. Captain Michaels had already warned us about what would happen if we got in another fight, and I didn't want to imagine what would be worse than kitchen duty. I continued to stare into John's eyes and saw the desperation lurking underneath.

"Two years," I replied quietly. My shoulders slumped forward with my confession and I saw the immediate flash of hurt and betrayal across his face.

John took a step back from me and straightened his back. His eyes were no longer on fire, but they had returned to the stormy gray I was familiar with when he was emotional. He reached out for the stack of letters, as if he needed to reread them to understand what was happening, but then his hand dropped to his side and remained there.

"Two years?" He said softly to himself. I—surprisingly— remained silent. He glanced back down at the letters, and I saw a discrete shudder course through him. Dan slid his right foot slowly and subtly toward John, positioning himself closer to him and away from me. I knew John had noticed Dan's movement and knew what he was preparing to do if necessary, but John didn't seem to care. John shook his head and stared at the letters.

"Does she love you?" he asked softly, finally grabbing the top letter he had been holding earlier and holding it delicately in his hands. I watched his motions and shook my head. We were both treading on unfamiliar ground; I had never witnessed him this upset—this emotional—in his life, and he had never wanted answers more than a beating before. It was difficult to gauge what to do, because we both knew each other so well; each of us knew exactly how the other would react.

I took a deep breath and gave him a verbal response, since he hadn't looked up from the letter in his hands.

"No, she doesn't. At least, not the way you mean," I said honestly.

John's brow furrowed slightly in confusion, but he didn't say anything. He gently brushed his fingers along the crisp paper where his mother's name was written in the upper left corner, and then down to where her scrawling writing curved around the letters that spelled out mine. He took in a shallow breath and nodded once.

"Do you love her?" he asked, following up his previous question just as quietly. I let out a breath and once again shook my head. John wanted answers I didn't have for him. The questions he was asking didn't have answers. I knew he saw me shake my head, this time from the way that his shoulders and forearms tensed. If I wasn't careful and I pushed the wrong button (as I had a tendency to do), he would lay my ass out flat and we'd all have the captain to answer to—or worse, the colonel.

"Not the way you mean, John," I said cautiously. John's hands gripped the letter roughly, and I could see the fragile paper tear under his angry fists.

"I don't understand," he said simply. I winced and nodded. All the times I had imagined telling him, all the times I had tried, and all the times Mrs. Cummings and I had discussed it—there had never been a clear way to answer that question.

July 1939

I lay on my back, staring at the clear night sky above me. A warm breeze ran over our exposed flesh and chilled the beads of sweat that had collected upon my chest and legs. Her curly blonde locks were soft against my skin where her head rested on my chest. Her breathing was just as heavy as mine, and we both just lay there for a moment in silence. I tried to think about how this had all come to happen; how walking her home from work in town on this dark summer night had led to this. I remembered meeting up with her, just as John had asked me to do. The Dragon had recently been released from jail, and we knew he was unhappy with her. He had been spotted at the bar, so we knew it was unlikely he would beat us home, but John didn't want to take any chances. We tried to persuade her to stay with a friend, stay with my family, stay at the motel—anything but go home. She refused and proclaimed that she could handle it. I gently ran my fingers through her soft hair as I continued to think. John couldn't walk her home, because he had a date with some girl from a nearby town named … hell I don't remember, but whoever she was, she was the reason I walked Mrs. Cummings home that night and not him. We had been talking, about nothing important, and then I didn't know what changed. Suddenly all the dreams I'd had since I started to notice women and how beautiful they were came true. I looked down at the woman in my arms with disbelief and happiness.

"I love you," I told her. My heart was pounding heavily from our lovemaking and from the excitement that coursed through me with uttering those words. I heard her laugh; it was a sweet sound like bells clinking. She lifted her head off of my chest and looked at me, the stormy gray clearing from her eyes.

"Oh, Ben," she said, sitting up and grabbing her blouse that had been discarded somewhere beside us. I watched as she pulled the thin, white fabric over her head and tugged it slowly over her breasts before tucking it into her black skirt.

I frowned a little and sat up, some of the grass I had been lying on sticking to my damp back. I shook my head a little to try to clear it, but I was still very confused. "I don't understand," I said to her, taking my shirt from her outstretched hand as she approached me.

She smiled, her lips no longer the bright red they had been when we left town, but the soft, natural pink that she always covered with lipstick. She sat down beside me and shoved one delicate foot into a low-heeled shoe, and then the other. I shook out my shirt in my hands and thrust it over my head, quickly pulling it down over my chest. She shook her head at me and grabbed my hand to hold between her two significantly smaller ones. "I know you don't," she said.

My brow creased further into confusion, and her smile broadened. She squeezed my hand reassuringly, and I knew I wasn't going to like whatever she had to say next. "You may think you love me now, with all the excitement coursing through your body, and for a moment it may be true, but then it will fade, and you will find that you're not in love with me at all."

I shook my head, still very confused at what she was getting at. Mrs. Cummings noticed and let out a deep sigh. "But I do love you," I said, clasping my other hand over hers. "I … I've never felt this way about you before. It's not the same; it's something more," I said, stammering in my confusion and inexperience at these kinds of conversations. She smiled at me and scooted closer to me in the grass.

"I know, Ben. I feel differently about you, too. You're right; it's not the same," she said sweetly. I started to smile and turn toward her, but she cut me off with a very commanding stare that told me to wait and listen before I made an idiot out of myself.

"But," she said slowly, dragging the word out between her white teeth, "you need to understand, Ben. I've always loved you. First I loved you as my son's friend, and now I love you as a man, but I will never love you as a husband. That's a different kind of love—a love that I've already pledged to a man."

My head was spinning from so many new emotions coursing through me. I quickly snatched my hands from her grasp and brought them to my temples. I was excited and blissfully happy when she told me she loved me, then hurt when she clarified what that love was, and now rage was rapidly taking over me when she confessed she actually loved the man that beat her and her child.

"You're telling me that you love me, but you don't really love me because you love that dick of a man?" I said, lowering one of my hands from my head and turning toward her.

She didn't flinch at my tone of voice; she never even moved back from my steadily tensing body. She just stared into me with those clear blue eyes and nodded. "You're not wrong about him. He is what you say. I've heard you and John calling him a dragon since you were kids, and I couldn't agree more."

I lowered my other hand and turned my entire body around to stare at her. "If you agree, then how can you love him?" I asked, trying to keep myself from yelling in disbelief and confusion.

She smiled but didn't move. Her body was still sideways to mine, and the only part of her turned toward me was her long, slender neck that I had just been trailing kisses down. "Because." She paused and pursed her lips in thought, and I could see that she was desperately trying to figure out how to explain this in a way that I would understand. "He wasn't like this when we first met; you must know that." She turned her torso more toward me. "We were young, and he was a gentleman. I was only sixteen when he asked my father for my hand. He was a hard worker; he had money and security to offer me. He owned land and a business." She paused, a small, ghostly smile on her lips. She lowered her eyes and looked at her hands, which began to smooth long tracks along her skirt. "I was only eighteen when I had John. He was still a good man; he took care of us. He loved me and his son very much." She looked sternly into my eyes to prove her point. Her hands stilled briefly on her skirt, and her tone became colder and harsher.

"Don't you doubt for a minute that he loved us, because he did. We had a good life until the market crashed. He lost everything: all his money, all his land, and his business just … gone. I know everyone suffered with the way the economy turned, but he took it personally. He told me that he failed us and that he was worthless. He tried to find work, he tried to rebuild the business, but it was impossible. He could get some labor jobs here and there and managed to bring home enough money to support us. I started working as an operator to help out, but he just took it as confirmation that he was a failure. That's when he started drinking. He barely touched the stuff before then, but now … he said it was the only thing that made him feel like he wasn't worthless." She took in a deep breath and shakily let it out. She turned away from me at this point and stared intently at the expansive dark sky stretched out above us.

"The first time he hit me, it was unexpected. I talked about it with my mother, and she just told me that a woman was supposed to support her husband. She told me I must've done something to offend him or insult him. She just smiled at me and showed me how to put powder on to cover it up." She lifted her head toward me, and I could see tears brimming in her eyes. I raised my finger to wipe them away but she just pulled back and took a deep breath. She blinked once and the tears were gone, and a hardened stoicism replaced them.

"I wanted to be a good wife; I wanted to be supportive," she said harshly. Her small hands clenched her skirt tightly. She took in another deep breath and loosened her grip on her skirt, smoothing out the wrinkles. She waited until her breathing was normal again, and she no longer showed any visible signs of frustration. She brought her knees up and leaned forward, resting her arms on her bent knees.

"The next time he hit me, I knew it wasn't in me to be the woman my mother had tried to make me be. I would be a supportive wife and mother, but I would not support him hurting me," she said bitterly.

I lifted my hand and slowly began to rub her back. "So why'd you stay with him if you felt that way?" I asked cautiously. Her story was kind of making sense to me, but everything she said only confirmed that she was not the type of woman to allow her husband to hurt her.

She brushed her yellow locks over her shoulder and looked back at me, her round shoulder blocking the lower part of her lips and chin from my view. "Because of John," she stated simply. I frowned in confusion, and my hand stalled its comforting circles on her back. I waited for her to explain further before I said anything. She turned back around and continued to lean on her bent knees.

"With the economy the way it is, I can't afford to take care of him on my own, and after having the man I love start to hurt me, well, I didn't exactly want to run out and find someone else to replace him. So I stayed. For a couple of years, he hurt only me, and as a wife I was angry, but as a mother I knew that this was the best life I could currently provide. He didn't start to hit John until he turned twelve, and that was only because John refused to let him hit only me. John provoked him to protect me." She paused, and once again I began to rub circles along her back to try to offer her some sort of comfort.

"I guess that makes sense, but how can you still love him?" I asked. I understood her reason for staying. She was right; she couldn't have been able to provide for herself and for John. But my mind couldn't grasp how, after everything she had just confessed, she could still love him. She smiled and turned back to look at me again.

"Because I still love the man I married. I don't love what he's become, and if you really want to know, I don't love him—this 'dragon,' as you call him. But I love my husband."

I frowned and tilted my head at her to show that I still didn't fully understand. "He's … not your husband?"

She smiled more broadly and shook her head at me. "I know it doesn't make much sense to you, but, I love my husband. My husband is the man I married. He is not that person anymore, even though legal documents say differently."

A warm feeling started to course through me, and I felt as if I had misunderstood the whole conversation. "So you could love me?" I asked with a giddy smile on my face.

Her smile slowly disappeared, and lines of pity replaced the dimples that had been there. She shook her head and turned to look at me straight on. I took in a sharp breath and held on to it. I had a not-so-great feeling about what she was going to say next.

She brought up her small hand and cupped my cheek, her thumb gently brushing the dark stubble on my jaw. "No, Ben. I told you, I can't love you like that, because I love my husband. He may not be that man anymore, but I still love the man that I lost. I will never be able to give you that love, because I already gave it to him. He may not be here anymore, and I constantly mourn him whenever I look at the beast that took his place, but I will always love the man I married." Her blue eyes stared into mine and cut through my heart.

I slowly nodded in understanding, and we stared at each other for a couple minutes in silence. "So why not leave him now that John's capable of taking care of himself?" I asked.

She just shrugged and continued to hold my face in her hand. "I can't disappoint and shame my family by getting a divorce, but you're right. Who knows, things may change. Accidents happen sometimes." She smiled at me and leaned forward, pressing her lips against mine. I smiled back and wrapped my arms around her, picking her up and pulling her onto my lap.

"So this was an accident?" I asked teasingly, nibbling her chin.

She laughed, and I felt the vibrations of it under my lips. "This was a total accident, to be sure," she said, tilting her head back so I could kiss her throat. I chuckled against her neck until she pulled away and brought my face up so that I was once again staring into her eyes.

"But you can't tell John about this," she said.

I snorted at her seriousness and pulled her hands away from my face. "Yeah, like I'm dumb enough to do that! He'd rip my head off!" I said.

She nodded in agreement. "I know, so if this is going to ever happen again, then he must never know," she said, her eyes cutting through me.

I nodded in understanding before my brain fully decoded her words. "Wait, happen again? But you just said you could never love me," I said, perplexed by the woman in my arms.

Mrs. Cummings laughed and kissed me again. "I know, and I can't. But that doesn't mean it's not nice to be with a man whom I care about, and who cares about me. I haven't had a man make me feel like a woman in a very long time. I need you, Ben. I need you to care about me, but I just don't need you to be in love with me."

I took in a deep breath through my nose and slowly let it out. I looked into those blue eyes and felt myself smiling. "I can do that," I said. I saw her smile briefly before I leaned in and kissed her again.

November 1941

John and I stared at each other, and I knew he was waiting for me to say something, to explain what he needed to know. I gazed back, knowing that if I lowered my eyes he would think I was lying, which would break what little restraint he currently had. It was strange for me to try to plan out my next move in a confrontation; usually I just said whatever came to mind that would push the right button to get the fists flying. I was never good at the talking part of any argument. I took a deep breath and tried to figure out what to say.

John's fiery eyes were unchanging as they watched my every move. His eyes were calculating, but without the usual detachment that they had when he was engaged in a battle. My shoulders slumped as I observed all the pain and betrayal in his eyes. All the times Mrs. Cummings and I were together, all the nights and secret afternoons we lay in each other's arms, I prayed that John would never find out. I knew that we should've stopped; I knew that it was wrong, and I always knew that one day he'd be looking at me just like he was right now. It was breaking my heart to see how I'd hurt him, to see all my lies swimming in his eyes, but I couldn't look away. For the first time in my life, I was at a loss for words. I didn't know what to say or where to begin. I broke the eye contact between John and me and looked over at Dan.

He was watching us both very closely, his dark eyes flicking back and forth, his square frame crouched and ready to break up a brawl. He looked at me from beneath his bushy eyebrows, and I could tell he was just as curious to hear my explanation.

"Fuck." Not the best word to say, not the smartest way to begin this conversation, but fuck, it was the only thing that I could force out. I took another deep breath and looked back at John. He was still tense, and he was still furious, but he had taken a step back, and I could tell that my response had thrown him a little off guard. He narrowed his eyes, and his lips tightened.

"Fuck? That's all you have to say?" he growled.

I shook my head and closed my eyes. I brought my hands up from where they were dangling at my sides to rub my forehead. I suddenly had a headache coming on, and I knew it was due to all this unusual thinking I was currently doing.

"John, you know I'm not good at this whole explaining myself thing. I … I just don't know where to begin. I don't know how to begin to tell you what you want to know." I dropped my hands and looked back at John. My arms hung limply at my sides, and I lowered my head—partially in shame, but mostly because my neck just couldn't seem to hold it up anymore. I saw John nod and slowly cross his arms, shifting his weight away from an attack posture to a—albeit intimidating—listening stance. He took a deep, calming breath in and nodded.

"So why don't you start at the beginning. How did this happen?" he asked smoothly. I brought my head up and watched him for a moment, analyzing his stance and the emotions in his eyes. Despite how angry and betrayed he felt currently, he was cutting me slack and walking me through the process of a confession. I watched him and tried to hold back the small smile I felt curving at my lips. Even in a confrontation that could possibly break our friendship—no, brotherhood—he was still taking care of me and making sure I didn't do something stupid. I knew that it was mostly instinctual and that he wanted to make sure he got all the answers he wanted before any bridges were irreparably burned, but it still gave me hope that I hadn't totally fucked up.

"It was an accident. I was walking her home from work one night, like you asked, and it just … happened," I said as clearly as I could.

John frowned and shifted his weight from his left leg to his right. "It 'just happened.' How does fucking my mother 'just happen?'" he asked, his jaw tensing with anger but the rest of his body remaining stationary. I marveled briefly at the extreme self-restraint that John possessed. It was a quality that I never had.

"I don't know, John. From what I remember, one minute we were looking at the stars and I was pointing out the big dipper and other constellations, and the next minute we were kissing and on the grass—"

"All right! I get it," he said with a wince. I nodded and closed my mouth, preventing any more words from escaping.

John began to rub his temples with one hand while the other remained protectively circled around his abdomen. "Knowing how you react to being surprised, I know that there's no way you remember who kissed who first," he said simply.

I nodded and looked down at my hands, which were flexing involuntarily, itching to have something to fiddle with, something to distract them from this situation.

"So whose idea was it to continue the … relationship?" he asked, choking out the question, struggling to get the last word out of his mouth. He looked a little sick; the pallor of his face was becoming more and more colorless with each question he asked.

"Hers," I said simply. I figured the shorter and more direct my answers could be, the better. John frowned in confusion but nodded as he accepted my answer. I looked down at my hands again to hide my glare from John. Judging by his reaction, he seemed to think it was all my idea and that I had convinced his mother to do it. My glare deepened at the thought. He should have known I wasn't smooth enough to pull that off, especially not with his strong-willed mother.

"I guess that makes sense," I heard him whisper. I glanced up at him from my bowed position. His eyes were no longer focused on mine, and he was biting his lower lip, deep in thought, as he processed what I was saying. I waited patiently for the next question, not knowing what to do or say in the contemplative and tense silence in between. Dan eased his stance and stood back up, no longer concerned that we were in imminent danger of a fight breaking out between us again, but he remained between us, clearly still cautious. The silence seemed to hang for hours, building my fear and anticipation for his next question that he was thinking so intently about.

"One last question," he said. His voice was quiet in volume, but the baritone quality of it was vibrating in my ears. Staring at me now was the John that I was so familiar with, the John that I had hurt, betrayed, and done everything I could to protect. I nodded and waited for his final question, praying it was something I could answer.

"Why did you do it?" I took a sharp breath and winced. I stared at John as he waited calmly and patiently for me to answer. I blinked and glanced at Dan, thinking back to the advice he had given me in the kitchen. I couldn't afford to lose John; I needed him, and I knew that my answer would determine if he would ever be able to forgive me. I tried to think of a way that would get John to understand what I was about to tell him, a way that would allow him to process what was going on in my fucked-up brain.

"You know how you feel about Red?" I said, noticing him tilt his head in confusion. He nodded silently and waited for me to continue. I licked my lips nervously and continued with the avenue I had chosen to convey my rationale. "How your hearts just connect and how you love her so unconditionally that you would do anything for her, even if it meant giving her up so that she could have what you think would be a better life? It's not, and you're dumb for doing it, but that's not the point." I paused to regather my thoughts. John glared at me but remained silent while I pushed forward. I had multiple points to make, so two birds with one stone and all that shit. If this was my last chance to speak to him as a friend, as a brother, then I wasn't going to hold back.

"Well, I've never had that, John. I've never felt that way about a woman before. I'm not like you, John. We know this. I'm an idiot that speaks his mind. I'm childish, and I have a tendency for starting fights and getting on people's nerves. I'm not a knight in shining armor like you. Girls don't just fawn over me like they do you, John. That's okay; a serious relationship is above my maturity level anyway. But the closest I've ever come to any of that is with your mom. She's the only woman that actually knows me, understands me, and accepts me. I did what I did because I … I don't know if I'll ever find what you and Red have. That is why you're a fucking dumbass for ignoring her and pushing her away!" My hands were balled into fists, and I was shaking them at John in determination, as if they could plead with him to hear what I was saying better than I could.

I let my words hang in the air between us and watched as he slowly soaked them into himself to ponder. We stared at each other for a while. My eyes were desperate and passionate with my speech, and his were just empty. As we stood there, I began to feel that natural energy of his, that unique spark that was indescribable, begin to pull away and fade.

His eyes lowered and stared at the stack of letters lying on the table—betrayal innocently wrapped up in paper and bound with a single piece of twine. He shook his head once; it was slight and almost unnoticeable. Still staring at the letters, he opened his mouth and dealt the final thrash that both sucked the air from my lungs and made me want to scream.

"I thought you weren't like me." He lifted his eyes from the letters to stare into mine. "I thought you didn't lie."

I winced and wished that I had the sense to explain everything, but I couldn't find the words. I couldn't find any words. He gave me a curt nod before turning around and walking stiffly out of the dining area. We all watched him leave, and slowly the dining area began to buzz with noise again. Jim and his section turned back to each other and began gossiping like the women they were. My eyes followed John's retreat until I couldn't see him anymore and the blackness of the island had swallowed him. Dan moved toward me and looked me over. I glanced around the dining area, my eyes slowly taking in all of the different sections and all the men sitting in there.

"Don't worry," Bill said tensely, not looking at me. "Only a couple of them were watching, and even less could hear what was bein' said." I nodded, my eyes still scanning the men at their tables. There weren't many left at this hour, and soon we were all going to have to retire.

"That's good," I said; I was sincerely glad to know that our humiliation was not public beyond the men at my side.

Sweet Gary just watched me with his large, innocent eyes, clearly trying to piece everything together in his overly technical mind. His eyes followed the path around the room that mine had just taken, and stopped on Jim and his section. Unexpectedly, Gary shoved against Bill, flung himself off the bench, and began storming toward Jim and his section. He was filled with rage, and his tiny frame was tense. He had his shoulders squared in a determined and intimidating posture. Dan and I spun around to watch as he quickly approached Jim.

Jim had a big smile on his face and was laughing at a joke one of his section members had cracked, no doubt concerning me being a motherfucker. Literally. Bill got off the bench and came to stand next to Dan and me, following Gary's every move with an overprotective gaze.

"Should we go get him?" Bill asked, concern lacing in his words. I looked to my side, and saw Dan deep in thought. I knew that he was just as worried as Bill was, but he was processing the best choice—something he was obviously far better at than I ever was.

"If we go over there too soon, they'll think he's a pussy, and that'll humiliate him. He's not like Ben, who's too much of a dumbass to get offended," Dan said, not taking his eyes off of Gary. I nodded and shrugged in agreement, and we stood there in silence, watching Sweet Gary grow some balls. Jim's smile faded when Gary came to stand in front of him, silencing his entire section.

"What do you want?" Jim asked easily, his cool manner both nonchalant and threatening at the same time. Gary's glare deepened, and he reached out and grabbed Jim's collar roughly, pulling him toward Gary's face, which was twisted with anger and disgust. Bill took a step forward to help Gary, knowing as well as I did that Jim was not a fair fighter.

Dan flung out his arm and prevented Bill from going any farther. "Wait; you'll know when he needs us," he said simply. Bill relaxed a little and took a step back, returning to his formation beside Dan and me.

"You fucking did this," Gary said, jerking Jim a little as he did so. Jim shoved Gary away from him, threw his legs over the side of the bench, and stood up to his full height. While he was shorter than John and me, he was quite a bit taller than Sweet Gary. Gary didn't even flinch at the man that was looming ominously over him—the same man that he had seen beat my ass, and the man that he had just pissed off. I was very proud of him in that moment.

"What?" Jim said, stepping closer to Gary.

Gary just looked up and continued glaring. "You told John about the letters," Gary said coolly, bringing up his small hands and placing them on Jim's large chest before shoving him backward. I saw Dan flinch, but he didn't make a move toward Gary. Jim took a step back to brace himself against the unexpected shove. His eyes widened in surprise, obviously just as shocked as the rest of us that Gary had actually pushed him. After the surprise washed over him, Jim's eyes narrowed and his lips thinned into an angry line. He stepped forward and lowered his head so he was eye-to-eye with Gary. They were so close that Jim's long, straight nose was almost touching Gary's cheek. Jim took in a sharp breath and blew it out angrily. Gary didn't flinch or even take a step back; he just raised his chin a little and met Jim's glare head-on.

"Don't blame me for your friends' little domestic spat. I didn't have anything to do with Ben's fuck-up," Jim said, letting out a gruff laugh at the end. His thin lips twitched at the corners and curled into a very cold grin. Gary's eyes dropped from Jim's, and he pursed his lips tightly together. His small back was taut, and his hands were clenched in fists at his sides. I watched his shoulders slump a little, and Jim's smile widened in sick satisfaction. Bill began to walk forward, a protective and angry strut in his walk. Jim's dark eyes rose from where they were burning holes into Gary's bent head, and it was in that brief moment—that moment when Bill was stalking toward Jim, ready to defend Sweet Gary; the moment when Jim cockily watched Bill making his way toward him—that Dan and I saw Sweet Gary pull his arm back and swing from his shoulder just like Dan had showed him. My eyes widened in shock as Gary's fist collided with Jim's cheek, forcing his head to swing forcefully to the right. Bill stopped walking and stood a few feet away, silently watching as Jim crumpled to the ground. Gary stood menacingly over Jim, who was gingerly touching his already bruising cheek.

"You may not be the cause of the argument, but you sure as hell exaggerated it. I don't know how you found out about Ben's letters, but I know it was you! You're the only selfish fucking dipshit that would think it was his fucking business!"

Jim looked up at Gary in complete shock. I felt my jaw drop involuntarily. Jim just lay on the ground, unable to retort. Even his men stood in stunned silence behind him.

"Well shit, Gary's got bigger balls than youse, Ben," Dan said in my ear with a snicker. "Jim was always the one standin' over you like that."

I snapped my jaw shut and glared at Dan. "That's 'cause I didn't have the element of surprise like Gary did. I mean look at him! You'd never guess that that kid could pack such a blow."

Dan just shrugged and did nothing to hide his amusement at the situation. I shook my head and looked back at Sweet Gary. The shock was wearing off quickly, and I could see the blood pooling in Jim's face. The redness began to crawl up his neck and bloomed on his cheeks. His dark hazel eyes squinted, his pupils shrinking and becoming beady. Dan stiffened beside me, and I knew that he, too, saw the danger that was coming Gary's way.

Gary stepped back a half step, his clenched fists rising pathetically, limply, in front of him. Gary was so focused on Jim, who was slowly rising to his feet, that he didn't notice the fist from one of Jim's men come flying toward his sweet face. There was a sick crack as the balled fist slammed into Gary's nose. Gary twisted from the force of the punch, blood streaming down his face from his broken nose. Gary brought his hands up to his face instinctively, cupping them around his nose and cradling the blood between his fingers.

That was all it took; we sprang into action. No one would damage Sweet Gary and get away with it! Bill let out an unintelligible howl and tackled the large man that had punched Gary. The two men went flying back and crashed into a table behind them, their force and weight causing the wooden bench to crack and break beneath the pressure. The large man took hold of Bill's shirt and shoved Bill off of him and onto the sand. The man rolled toward Bill and swung back with a thick arm, slamming it into Bill's square jaw. Bill growled and swung his balled-up fist into the man's torso. The man grunted in pain and loosened his hold on Bill long enough for Bill to fling the man off of him and onto the already broken corners of the table.

The man yelped as the splintered wood jabbed him painfully in the small of his back. Bill scrambled to his knees, his breath coming out in heavy pants as he pushed his large frame up. The man pushed himself off of the broken table, swaying slightly on his heavy legs. Bill swung his arm back and threw his punch right when the man pitched forward in an attempt to regain his unsteady balance. The man's head followed the punch, with bloody spittle flying from his mouth as he was thrown backward onto the table, unconscious.

After Bill charged the man, Dan flung out his hairy arm and shoved me out of his way as he ran for Gary. I didn't think a shove was necessary, but I guess Dan just had a flair for the dramatic. Dan seemed to be running toward Gary as if he were in a haze and the only thing he saw was the boy. Some of Jim's men attempted to halt Dan by stepping in front of him, but Dan just wildly swung his fists at anything that got between him and Gary. One man managed to duck the flying fists and grabbed Dan around his waist, pushing him back. Apparently, Bill wasn't the only former football star in this tussle.

The short, stocky man shoved Dan until they collided with Jim's other man, who had not been so lucky to escape Dan's fists, resulting in a split eyebrow and busted lip. The tall, thin, bleeding man grunted as he lost his balance and collapsed into the sand, letting out a yelp as Dan and the stout man fell on top of him in a heap of flailing limbs.

Dan grabbed the stout man's thick, curly blond hair and yanked his head back. The stout man let out a cry of pain and lifted himself off of Dan to make the angle he was being pulled in less awkward. Dan swung his leg up and kicked the stout man in the gut, letting go of the man's curly hair as he did so in order to push the man's frame off of him. The stout man gagged and choked in an attempt to get air back into his lungs. Dan elbowed the squirming, bleeding, tall man crumpled beneath him and then shoved himself back onto his feet.

After Dan had shoved me unnecessarily out of his way (which I wasn't really in to begin with, but whatever), I noticed that Jim was still standing in front of Gary, a slight smile on his lips as he watched the crimson blood ooze out of Gary's broken nose. I felt fury, hot and burning, course through me at the sight of that bastard still standing. I made my way toward Jim, jumping backward so that when Dan was tackled I was not taken down with him, the stout man, and the tall bleeding guy.

While the three of them were struggling, I leapt over their thrashing limbs and continued toward Jim. First he had told John about my letters and their existence, breaking the bond I shared with the only man I would ever dare call my brother, and then he had smiled as poor Gary got his face punched in. My hands were sweating as I clenched them into tight fists. I glanced over my shoulder when I heard the stout man cry out, and I watched Dan kick him backward. I continued to watch Jim as I approached, and I noticed that while his thin lips were turned up in a smirk of satisfaction, his dark eyes held a hint of concern for the bleeding youth in front of him. Continuing forward, I reached Jim the same time that Dan reached Gary. When Dan reached Gary he was hunched over and letting the blood drip onto the sand, no longer cupping it in his hands.

Dan slowly raised Gary's head and analyzed the damage done to his previously straight nose. "All right, kid, hold still. This is gonna hurt, but it'll make sure ya can still breathe in and out of that pretty nose of yers." He tilted Gary's head backward a little and braced an index finger on either side of the bridge of Gary's nose. He then slowly pushed Gary's nose back into place, keeping it aligned with his thick fingers until it was nice and straight again. Gary let out a small cry, and tears leaked out of his eyes as Dan expertly fixed him.

"I know," said Dan. "Believe me, this is not my first time resettin' a broken nose. I've done it myself plenty of times, and look how fantastic I look!" Gary let out a gargled laugh and kept his head tilted back. Dan smiled and patted him on his slim shoulder. "Come on, kid. I got some tape back in my tent that we can put on it to help hold it in place while it heals." Gary didn't say anything but allowed Dan to guide him away from the brawl, where Jim's men were lying in crumpled heaps of bruised, bloodied, and groaning flesh.

Jim and I paid no attention to Gary and Dan exiting the aftermath. Bill stood somewhere behind us, away from his unconscious opponent and Dan's beaten men. I knew that Bill remained for support in case he was needed; he went and sat off to the side where he could recuperate from wrestling the large man.

Jim and I continued to analyze each other, neither one willing to break eye contact or speak first. As I noticed that Jim's eyes were not filled with fury but trepidation, I realized that I'd been staring into a lot of guy's eyes recently, which was a little strange to me. First it was John, and now this ass bag, but regardless, it proved to be effective in figuring out my next move. I wanted so badly just to punch his fucking face, but noticing the purple swelling that was developing on his cheek, I knew that not only had Gary beaten me to it, but also that he probably got a better hit in than I ever could.

106

Damn him and his tiny fists of surprise. It was impressive, though. I stared at Jim a while longer, and it hit me—he was waiting for me to say something before he made any move.

I looked around at his men lumped on the ground and Bill sitting a little ways off, rubbing his cheek. For the first time, without John's noble presence behind me commanding it, I had the upper hand. I felt my lips twitch briefly into a small smile of satisfaction before it crumbled. I looked back at Jim's uncertain yet bold and calculating eyes. I felt myself grow cold; the anger I had been feeling while walking toward him was freezing and falling like a rock in my stomach.

"It would be easier for me to hit you right now," I said, my voice deep and low.

Jim met my eyes and refused to look away, knowing that doing so would mean admitting that I intimidated him, and the prick had too much pride for that. "So why don't you just ball up and do it?" he asked, forcing his voice to sound angry and biting, but I knew that it was just a façade for the guilt that kept washing over his face. A part of me wanted to smile at that, but I suppressed it.

"Because I don't think you fully comprehend what you've done," I said. "Somewhere in your ass-backward way of thinking, I figure you thought you were getting back at me—or proclaiming your undying love and desire for me; I can't be too sure when it comes to you." I noticed Jim's jaw clench; the muscles twitched a little, but he remained silent and didn't retort. I raised a curious eyebrow and nodded slightly before continuing. Usually Jim wouldn't let me get away with a comment like that; usually it would push one of his overly sensitive buttons. I guess this time he really was going to let me do all the talking. Huzzah!

"John's my brother, or the closest thing I've got to one," I said.

"So that's why you fucked his mother?"

I swung my left arm and punched his other, untouched cheek. "Don't interrupt, or I'll make sure you don't just have matching purple cheeks, but a couple of black eyes, too." I stared coldly at Jim as he brought up a hand and tenderly prodded his right cheek. He just pursed his lips, narrowed his eyes in a meaningless glare, and let his hand fall back to his side, letting me know I should continue.

"As I was saying, before I was so crudely and rudely interrupted, he's the closest I have to a brother, and you, because of your sick sense of self-entitlement, felt it was your fucking business to get involved with our issues. You, you twisted ass-bitch, hurt my brother because you didn't understand when to butt out." I roughly reached out and grabbed hold of his shirt and pulled him toward me. Jim's eyes widened in surprise, but he remained silent. I felt the anger begin to burn again and melt me from the inside out.

"I don't know what it was you were thinking you'd accomplish, you sack of shit, but I can assure you, you have failed," I growled and felt my teeth grind in fury. As I stared into his eyes, which were desperately trying to conceal their guilt with tides of pride, I felt a rage wash over me as I never had before. Because of the man I held in my fists right now, John was suffering from a pain and betrayal that I had been trying to shield him from for two years until I knew how to break it to him easy. Because of the weasel in my grasp, the person who had always been there for me—who would kill for me, and whom I would die for—might never want to be a part of my life again. Admittedly, it was right for John to feel that way, and it was all my fault, but at the time, with Jim in my hands—considering all my mistakes and the dawning understanding of the depth of the situation washing over me and drenching me in its freezing reality— it was easier to blame Jim and his big mouth.

I shook Jim a little, the rage pouring out of my core and into my arms. Jim closed his eyes in anticipation of the inevitable blow. I wanted to hit him. I wanted to beat him. I wanted to kick him in the ribs and break his nose and inflict upon him all the wounds that had ever been inflicted upon me. In one of the only moments of clarity that I've ever had, while staring into the proud face of Jim, with his tan skin, clenched jaw, and tightly closed eyes, I knew that even if I beat him to a bloody pulp, it wouldn't change anything. It would only get me into more trouble with Captain Michaels, and I didn't really want to know what was worse than kitchen duty. The immense anger that had burned in me slowly sizzled out and left me with the one thing I really wanted from Jim: not his blood, not his pain, not even his wussy baby tears, but just an answer.

"Why'd you do it?" I asked, gently pushing him away from me and releasing the fabric of his shirt.

Jim slowly opened his eyes and looked directly into mine. "What's it matter at this point?" he asked. His voice was low and steady, and his back was straight. I pondered that for a moment before I simply nodded my head calmly and slammed my fist into his left eye.

"I guess it doesn't."

♦♦♦

I couldn't stand to be around anyone after what had happened in the dining area—first my confrontation with John, and then the brawl between our section and Jim's. None of my friends said anything (they never would), and while it was reassuring to know they still had my back, their silent judgement was burning me. I just needed space, so I went to the only place where I knew I could get some: the beach. I had notified the night watch that I was there and gave them some rolls that I had pilfered from the kitchen earlier that day. They had accepted the snack and left me alone to stare at the stars.

I was thankful to see their familiar celestial bodies twinkling and shining down on me. At least I could always count on these heroes never leaving me. As I stared up at Orion, the hunter, and Perseus, the savior and defender of Andromeda, I felt shame wash over me. I didn't know how long I had expected to keep my relationship with Mrs. Cummings a secret from John. I didn't know how I thought I'd tell him, or when, if ever. I thought of all the nights that she and I had lain together, a sweaty heap in each other's arms. And in those brief moments when we lay there silently together, I felt complete. I knew it wasn't the love that John had with Red, or even close to that. I knew it wasn't the love that Mrs. Cummings had for her husband before he became the monster. But it was a type of love. It was a kind of love between the two of us, consisting of simple understanding and acceptance. She may have been his mother, but she was my friend.

I stared up at my heroes, and the shame I previously felt washed away. They weren't perfect either; they'd fucked up plenty of times, and yet they were still found worthy enough to be immortalized in the heavens. I stared at my hunter and warrior and knew that even though it was wrong, and I was paying the price for my actions, I wouldn't have taken back a moment that I had spent in Mrs. Cummings's arms.

I took out the pen and paper I'd brought with me and began to write a letter to her, the stars my only source of illumination. I began with some babble about daily life and how much I wished I could be home with her right now, and eventually I led into the most important four words I could have ever told Mrs. Cummings: "John knows about us."

◆ ◆ ◆

I spent the night in Gary's tent again, knowing that John had no interest in seeing me anytime soon. I really couldn't blame him; if the tables were reversed, I'd be pretty sore with him, too. I hadn't gotten very far in my letter to Mrs. Cummings the night before. It was too dark, and I had only been able to explain the fight John and I had gotten into about Red. I figured I'd finish the letter that night and send it off with the mail the following week.

At breakfast I remained silent, listening to Bill and Dan as they fawned over Gary's broken nose and told him he should write his girl and tell her what a stand-up guy he was for defending his friend. Gary just chuckled and shook his head. He had a piece of tape stuck over the bridge of his nose to hold it in place while it healed, and I could tell that it bothered him, because he kept touching the corners of the tape gingerly. Dark purple and blue streaks stretched out across his face like a spider, all of them leading to the large purple mass that was his damaged nose. I could tell that Sweet Gary was in pain, but like a trooper, he stuck it out and did his best not to let on. There were no other mentions about the events of last night, but I could still see their judging sideways looks at me, but they said nothing since they were just as determined as me to carry on normally. As we sat there eating our breakfast, I saw the last person on that sand bar that I wanted to see walking toward us. I groaned, alerting the other three of his mobilizing presence.

"Privates!" the captain said, his voice booming. We quickly shuffled out of our seats and stood alert in front of him. He scanned us all slowly; his eyes squinted in menacing analysis.

"Swanson! What the hell happened to you?"

Gary swallowed roughly before confidently responding. "Sir, I fell and broke my nose."

Captain Michaels stared at him for a moment, his eyes still squinted as if he was contemplating whether or not he should accept this answer. "There have been a lot of accidents happening recently. It seems the entirety of Connor's section had a variety of them yesterday as well." Captain Michaels took a deep, intimidating breath in through his nose and released it slowly. To Gary's credit he didn't flinch or falter in any way. He was certainly a better liar than I ever was.

"All right, to avoid getting Major Devereux involved, it had better been just a fall. Are there going to be any more accidents happening with this section?" Captain Michaels stared each one of us down, his silver eyes turning cold and sending a chill through me. I already had kitchen duty, and the last thing I wanted was to get the major involved.

"No, sir. We will be more careful and make sure there will be no more accidents," I said.

Captain Michaels turned back to me and stared at me a moment before nodding curtly. "Good. You have your assignments from yesterday; get to it." He then stiffly walked away. Once he had disappeared from the dining tent, we all relaxed and sat back down.

"Ya did good, kid," Bill said in commendation to Gary, patting him roughly on the back. Dan nodded in agreement and continued eating. There wasn't much conversation after the captain's interruption, and we quickly finished and split up to go back to our assigned punishments. As I collected the trays, I scanned the remaining men, trying to find a familiar head of blond hair and blue eyes, but he wasn't there. I nodded to myself and followed Dan quietly to the kitchens. As we entered the humid, dark lair and stacked all the dirty dishes by the cleaning tubs, Dan finally spoke to me.

"So last night was interesting," he said.

I snorted at his word choice and continued to roll my sleeves up. "That's a fuckin' understatement, but sure, let's go with interesting." I grabbed the first dirty dish beside me and began to scrub it in the soapy water, careful not to slosh any water onto the sand.

Dan grabbed the nearest pot to begin cleaning. "All right, all right. Last night was a fuckin' disaster. Are ya gonna try to talk to John?" His question came out muffled and with a slight echo as he

111

bent over the pot to scrub a particularly stubborn spot. I sighed and grabbed another plate. I should've known I wasn't going to have a great day where I could pretend the previous night hadn't happened. Stupid Dan and his desire to help by digging deep into my problems so that they can get resolved, I thought. "I'm not sure. John usually likes some time to himself after a fight." I started to think back to every fight we'd ever had. John always kept to himself for a day or two before he'd talk to me again. I was usually over it a lot faster than he was, but John tended to hold on to things a lot longer than I did.

"He may not seem like it," I said, for some reason feeling like I needed to explain John to Dan, "but John is a very emotional kind of guy." It was as if I thought an understanding of John and his process would help Dan understand why this situation was so delicate—not that the details he was privy to didn't already make that clear.

Dan turned to look at me, his thick arms still scrubbing the pot in his hands.

"That's not to say he's a pansy and cries all the time or anythin'," I said, "but he does have a deep emotional connection to people and events—more than anybody I've ever met. He takes everythin' personally, and if you wrong him, he'll never forget it." I looked up from my soapy hands and over to where Dan was standing listening.

Dan just nodded and pursed his lips. "Well, it's not like many guys would be forgettin' a thing like that. Youse got as personal as youse can get," he muttered. I looked away ashamed but he didn't add anything more to it. I glanced back up at him and could tell from the way his brow was furrowed and his eyes were hidden beneath the bushy masses above them that he was absorbing what I told him.

"What's the worst fight youse two have ever had, before this?" Dan asked. I took a moment and really thought about it. To be honest John and I hadn't had too many fights. That's not to say we never disagreed or did stupid things to each other, but we rarely fought. I usually caved in to prevent a brawl, but there were a couple of times when I didn't back down.

July 1933

"You're doing it wrong!" I shouted, pushing John's hands away and taking the seeds and trowel from him. John glared at me and tried to take his tools back, but I shoved him off and continued digging a trench for the seeds and sprinkling them along the line of soil I had revealed for them. John's adolescent hands grabbed mine and yanked the tools out of them, sending the remaining seeds flying.

"Now look what you did!" he said, glaring at me and grabbing another bag of seeds to repeat what I had just shown him one row over.

I scoffed, my fourteen-year-old pride flaring up, and pushed him roughly in the shoulder. "What I did? I was planting them correctly before you messed me up!" I shoved him again. John scoffed and flung his arm out to push me backward while he kept planting the seeds. I took his arm and pulled him backward toward me.

"You're still doing it wrong! Those seeds need to be sown in little pockets of dirt!" I shouted. John wiggled on top of me, trying to get me to release him. He grunted and slammed his elbow backward into my ribs. I immediately released him and groaned, holding my bruised side. I looked up at him and saw uncertainty in his eyes as he tentatively scooped a large clump of dirt onto one of the seeds. I groaned and sat up, shaking my head. I let go of my tender ribs and reached out and showed him how to wrap the seed in a small handful of dirt and cover it gently. John didn't say anything and began to mirror my actions with the remaining seeds.

"Why can't you just admit that I might know something that you don't?" I asked, watching him packing the dirt around the seeds we were planting for his mother's garden. Mrs. Cummings had recently been over at my house, had seen my mother's own garden, and had decided that she, too, wanted fresh vegetables and herbs on hand. Mrs. Cummings didn't have any time to actually plant the garden herself, though, because she was busy working. Since it was the summer, John had naturally volunteered our services to help out his mom. I didn't mind that he volunteered me to do gardening work; I was used to doing it for my own mother, and I would do anything for Mrs. Cummings. What I did mind was that he wouldn't listen to me when I clearly knew what I was talking about.

"Come on, John! Why do you always have to know more than me?" I shouted. John remained silent and grabbed another bag of seeds. Very rarely did I feel it necessary to push his buttons, but I was really sick of him acting as though he was better than me.

"You think you know more than me? You think you're better than me just because you have to help me in a few fights? Well that's bullshit!" I pushed myself off of the dirt and gave him a shove as I stood up.

John threw down the trowel and bag of seeds, standing too. "A few fights? Try every fight your big mouth has gotten you in! And I don't think I'm better than you; how dare you say that!" he yelled back at me, his longish blond hair falling into his eyes, partially hiding me from his view. He brought up his hands and pushed me back. I stumbled but caught myself before I tripped over the pitchfork we had borrowed from the Millers to clear out growth and make way for the garden.

"I don't ask for your help, John! You act like you're better than everyone else, not just me, and we all know that you're not. Just because your daddy kicks your ass doesn't mean you have to fight the whole world!" Immediately after the words left my mouth, I wanted to take them back. I wanted to pluck them out of the air and eat them as if they had never left my mouth. His blue eyes turned a stormy gray and he let out a growl before grabbing the collar of my shirt and throwing me into the dirt. We began to wrestle, trying to pin each other to the dirt so we could get in a punch or two. We rolled around, getting the soft soil and sharp grass pressed into our clothes, undoubtedly leaving stains.

"What is goin' on here?" we heard someone shrilly shout from somewhere above us. We paused in our abuse and looked up to see Mrs. Cummings standing over us. She had dropped the grocery bag that she had been holding and crossed her arms. Her face was twisted into an angry scowl, and she glared at us, wrapping us in disappointment and guilt. "I'll ask again. What is going on?" she said, her foot beginning to tap in agitation. I pushed myself off of the ground and tried to dust myself off, while John just lowered his head.

"Sorry, Ma," John said softly. "We were arguing, and it got out of hand." I turned and looked at the ruined bed of dirt behind us. The seeds that had been successfully planted were now tossed all over and no longer in the neat rows that they had been in. I looked up at her and saw tears brimming in her eyes. I couldn't tell if the tears were from sadness or anger, but I really didn't want to find out either way.

"We'll fix it, ma'am. I promise," I said, and I dropped to my knees and began sorting the seeds. John looked up and into his mother's eyes, remaining still and silent.

Mrs. Cummings pursed her lips, and her jaw tightened a little. "Those seeds were expensive and very hard to get. We don't have much land to try and produce food, but if we can, then maybe we can help out the Millers; they are really struggling on their farm."

John nodded and looked down again in shame. I looked over my shoulder and watched as Mrs. Cummings took a couple steps forward to stand in front of her son. She took his awkwardly large hands into her small, petite ones and urged his eyes to look into hers. "I know it's hard right now. Your father's not doing much work, and I'm gone all the time trying to earn some money for us. Times are hard right now, but they'll get better. You're very strong, John. I need you to keep being strong." John nodded. I looked away, knowing that this was a very private and vulnerable moment that I shouldn't bear witness to. I heard Mrs. Cummings whispering more words of encouragement to her son, and I pictured her sweet smile as she did so. I could hear the gentle rumble of John's deepening voice as he responded to her, but I couldn't quite make out the words.

Not too much longer after John spoke to her, he returned to my side and watched me finish sorting the seeds we had mixed up. "What now?" he asked softly and tersely. I looked over at him and noticed that he was very stiff and staring intently at the seeds before him. Without saying anything, I scooped up the first pile of seeds and showed him how to plant them correctly.

I glanced over my shoulder and saw Mrs. Cummings smiling. As she walked toward us, her foot kicked the long handle of the pitchfork. Her smile faded, and her face twisted in confusion. "Where'd you get this?" she asked, bending down and picking it up. She stared inquisitively at the prongs and twirled it in the afternoon light.

"The Millers. It was Ben's idea that we get it to clear out all the weeds and dead stuff," John said. I lifted my head and smiled at him, glad that he was giving me credit for one of my few brilliant ideas. John smiled back and took another seed from my open hand.

Mrs. Cummings had a smile in her voice when she responded. "That was a great idea, Ben. You boys be careful, though; it's awfully sharp." And with that last motherly warning, she walked away, letting us finish planting the seeds.

November 1941

I put the recently cleaned dish on the steadily growing pile of shiny dishware and reached for another. Dan nodded quietly to himself and continued washing as well. His lips twitched, and he frowned a little in confusion.

"So that's the worst fight youse two have ever had?" he asked. He scoffed and turned to face me, crossing his thick, hairy arms across his wide chest. "If that's the worst you've ever had, then youse guys' relationship is remarkable! I'm surprised one of ya didn't snap earlier," He chuckled; the vibrations made his arms bounce on his chest.

I shook my head and set aside the dish I was working on. "No, that wasn't the worst. That was the start of the worst fight we ever had, which happened two years later when we were sixteen."

Dan stopped his chuckling and tilted his head inquisitively to one side. "All right, so what's the worst then?" he asked, making a sweeping gesture with his arm for me to elaborate. I took a deep breath in and let it out with an exasperated puff. If I told Dan what our biggest fight was about, then he'd know John's biggest secret. The secret that was the source of John's pride and shame. Dan stood there, waiting expectantly for me to continue. I blew out another puff of air and walked toward him so that we were no longer talking across the kitchen.

"If I tell you this story, then I need you to promise that no one— and I mean no one, not even Bill or Gary, and especially not John—

finds out that I told you." I waited for Dan to give me his confirmation, and I stared at him intently until he did. I needed to make sure that John's secret didn't get around to any more ears than what I was willing to divulge it to.

Dan lifted his right hand and grasped my own in a tight shake. "Ya have my word. I'll take it to my grave."

I shook his hand then, and true to his word, that's exactly what he did.

September 1935

John and I were sitting on my front porch, watching the sun trek across the morning sky until it was directly overhead and beating down upon us. We had gone into town earlier to try to find some work for that day, but there was none to be had. Many of the farms were drying up, thus not needing any hands to help, and the shops already had a surplus of people wanting to work in them. We sat in silence for god knows how long before John looked up from the book in his hands.

"You're going to ruin those pretty eyes of yours if you keep staring at the sun like a moron," he said to me.

I smiled and kept my head tilted toward the sky, watching the tops of the trees sway gently in the almost nonexistent afternoon breeze. "Nah, I'd rather keep staring at the sky than at some book," I replied.

John snorted and turned back to the bound pages in his calloused grip. He picked up the book and shoved the cover in my face so I could see nothing but the printed letters of the author's name and the title of the book. "This is fascinating. This is classic literature. This—"

"Is a dead guy sobbing on and on about his equally dead friend," I said, and I roughly shoved the book out of my face. John glared at me and held the book up again, but at a farther distance from my face. "What a horrible way to describe such beautiful words," John said to me.

I rolled my eyes and continued to stare at the treetops, their leaves beginning to change color in the cooling autumn air. "Yeah I get it. Tennyson's legendary, the queen adored him and la-di-da. I hope you're using this bullshit to impress the girls in town like that Maggie Miller. I hope knowing Tennyson gets you a throw with her." I snorted and started laughing at my own joke.

John scoffed and turned away from me. "Why do you always have to make everything about that?" he said angrily. "Can't you just enjoy something without making it be about that? And no, I'm not using it to impress girls. I happen to like reading it."

I rolled my eyes again and rested my chin on the palm of my hand. "Sure. Reading about an old dead guy sobbing on and on is loads of fun," I said sarcastically.

John whipped around in his chair and faced me, his brow furrowed and his eyes angry. "You know, maybe if you read a little more you wouldn't be such an idiot, Ben."

I flinched at his tone and looked at him incredulously. "I did read it! I read it a month ago when you first shoved it in my face and told me it was the best fucking thing you'd read this year. I told you a week later when I finished with Tennyson's sob-ass story that I hated it. What crawled up your bum hole?"

John just tightened his jaw and twisted forward so he was no longer facing me but the yard. I couldn't quite figure it out. We had been having a lovely morning before he went and got all moody for no reason. Sometimes John would be as stable as a tree, and then other days he'd be as emotional and whacked-out as my mother when she got her menses.

I turned back to my trees and let out a huff of frustrated air. "You've been acting like a goddamn broad ever since you tried to beat the Dragon and got your ass kicked three months ago," I said under my breath. Apparently I wasn't as quiet about my musing as I had hoped I was, because the next thing I knew, John was yanking me from my chair and throwing me down the porch steps. I hit the dry dirt, and it flew up angrily around me in a cloud. John came stomping down the steps and grabbed my collar before I could push myself up. He pulled back his arm and punched me square in the nose, causing me to cry out in pain. John withdrew slightly, and his grip on my collar loosened as he stared at me in shock, as if he couldn't believe what he had just done. I brought my hands down from my bleeding nose and took the opportunity to punch him back.

"What the hell, John!" I exclaimed. He stumbled backward from the force of my punch and fell into the dirt across from me. He glared at me from under the blond hair that fell into his eyes. Once I realized that he wasn't going to attack me again, I went back to nursing my bleeding nose. I tilted my head back and pinched the bridge in an attempt to get it to stop bleeding. I kept my head tilted back and looked over at John. "Goddamn it, man! Taking me out isn't going to suddenly make you feel better. You aren't suddenly a hero because you threw my punk ass down some stairs! He's the one you're pissed at. I know you're sore about what happened, but shit, don't take it out on me!" My nose started to bleed again from the amount of adrenaline coursing through me. I watched John cautiously, uncertain if he was going to take another swing at me.

John looked away from me, and I saw his face begin to twist in anger. He slammed his fists into the dirt, stirring up clouds of dust. I watched him for a minute more before I pushed myself off of the dirt and went to sit on the porch steps. I lowered my head when my nose had finally stopped bleeding and just watched as John pushed himself up and angrily paced back and forth.

"That bastard doesn't deserve to fucking breathe!" John screamed in fury. I just sat there and watched him. Well, at least he wasn't mad at me anymore.

November 1941

Dan just stared at me in stunned silence. I nodded to myself, confirming what I had just told him. Dan opened his mouth as if to speak, but then closed it and brought his hand up to cover his thick lips. He stroked his chin absently in thought for a couple of silent minutes before finally speaking.

"So ... that's where that scar actually came from?" Dan asked tentatively. I nodded and stared ahead, my eyes not focusing on anything in particular. He nodded along with me, everything clicking into place and understanding falling over him.

"Well, it doesn't seem like either of those fights lasted too long. The first one when youse guys were fourteen wasn't too bad, and he just didn't talk to you much for two days. The one when you were sixteen sounds like it was over in about fifteen minutes!" Dan let out a dry chuckle and pushed away from me to continue working. Lunch had just ended, so we had a new load of dirty dishes to clean. I crossed my arms and remained by his tubs.

"That's because we got in a fight with his Dragon and he got stabbed and I shot—well I tried to shoot—his Dragon to save him! So unless I can do somethin' similar this time around, I don't see him forgivin' me anytime soon," I replied huffily.

Dan paused for a second while he contemplated my answer, and then he went back to scrubbing. "Well, ya never know. I say we've got three more days of this shit, and that should give him plenty of time to cool down so youse can talk to him."

I shook my head and rolled my eyes before strolling back to my tubs of soapy water and beginning to wash plates again. Well, here's to being optimistic, I thought as I dunked a plate in the lukewarm water.

◆ ◆ ◆

I'm so sorry that I got us into this mess. I wouldn't take back a moment of what we had together, but it is clear that it's time to end it. I wish this didn't have to be through a letter. You don't know how badly I wish that I could be there with you right now but—

"Hey, whatchya writin'?" Gary asked as he plopped down on the bench next to me. I quickly stopped writing and folded the letter, hoping the ink wouldn't smudge. I would've finished this letter a week before, but it turned out to be a lot harder to write than I anticipated. Oftentimes I ended up just sitting and staring at the pen in my hand instead of actually writing anything down. I wasn't any good with words. It didn't matter how many poets or theorists John made me read; my brain just didn't work that way. Gary just smiled at me mysteriously but didn't press it.

"How's it goin', Gary?" I asked nonchalantly. Gary's smile got wider and more eager as he swung around on the bench so he was straddling it and facing me directly. My eyes widened briefly in surprise, because I wasn't expecting him to get so excited over such a simple question.

"Well! You know how Bill and I have been on guard duty for the past week while you and Dan have been in the kitchens?" he asked. I nodded in confirmation that I indeed knew what he was talking about. Our week of punishment and discombobulated section members was finally over, and I was preparing to take Dan's advice and try to talk to John. Just as I had predicted, he hadn't said a word to me. In fact, he hadn't even come near me since the night he found the letters. I saw him every now and then in the dining tent during mealtime, but he always ate by himself and left quickly. I was still working on the letter to send to Mrs. Cummings. I wrote it and rewrote it, but I just couldn't seem to get it right. I pulled the unfinished letter closer toward me and turned my attention back to Gary, who was bouncing eagerly like a child.

"It's been amazing!" Gary said. "We've had the chance to talk to a bunch of the guys that patrol those parts when our section doesn't have guard duty, and they have some of the most interesting stories!" Gary continued to excitedly babble about the guys and all the stories that they had told Bill and him. I must admit that, judging by the stories that I was actually paying attention to, they sounded like some interesting guys. Gary kept on rambling about his new patrol buddies when Dan and Bill showed up.

Dan sat down, his large hands grasping a few letters, and began to listen intently, trying to figure out what Gary was talking about. Bill sat down next to Dan, and after listening to what Gary was talking about, Bill quickly joined in, editing and commenting on Gary's retelling.

"No, no, Gary, it was Doug's truck that took out the water tower," said Bill. Then, "That's right! And he showed us the scar and it was just as nasty as he said." And during another story, "It never occurred to me what it would be like to kiss a man, but in that situation there's really nothin' else ya could do."

I narrowed my eyes in confusion at Bill's last comment and turned to see Dan's reaction. Dan was solemnly nodding his head in agreement along with Gary, which only confused me more, but I just shrugged it off and figured that's what I got for only half listening. The conversation only got stranger from there, but no matter how hard I tried to focus on the story about the hermaphroditic prostitute a guy named Carl had encountered, my mind and my eyes kept drifting to the letters that Dan casually gripped in his hands.

At one point, Dan lifted the letters up when he was enthusiastically gesturing about something Bill had said, and I instantly recognized Mrs. Cummings's scrawl. In that moment, my breathing increased and I wanted so desperately to rip the letters out of Dan's hairy hand. I tried to be discrete in my longing for the letters, laughing when the guys laughed and avoiding staring at the letters head-on. Instead I focused intently on each of the guys, staring obsessively at Gary's bright hair, Bill's round eyes, and Dan's large nose. Try as I might, I don't think I was as subtle as I wanted to be, because pretty soon Dan started fanning himself with the letters, or moving them up to his hairline to push his hair back or wipe his forehead. My eyes involuntarily followed the letters with each hand gesture Dan made, hoping that one of those gestures would end with him either dropping them or handing them over to me.

"Whaddya think about that, Benny?" Dan asked me, jerking me out of my obsessive letter watching. I quickly assessed all of the guys' current facial reactions and found them to be less than helpful. Gary had a slight nondescript smile on his patiently awaiting face, Bill looked curious and had his eyes narrowed in anticipation, and Dan had a smug toothy grin on his ugly mug, which I wanted to punch badly.

I nodded and cleared my throat. "Uh, yeah, sure," I said, nodding uncertainly. It wasn't soon after the words had left my lips that I realized that was not the right answer. Bill's face quickly twisted in disgust, and his brown eyes looked me up and down as if a disturbing personal fact had just been exposed. Gary winced, and his eyes just stared at me pityingly while he slowly shook his head from side to side. Dan, the asshole, just started laughing hysterically. Well, crap.

"So you're sayin'," Bill said, leaning forward with apprehension, "that you'd let a parrot eat a melon off of yer gonads?"

I stared at Bill incredulously for a minute, my brain rapidly trying to remember the bits of the conversation that I had heard, but for the life of me, I couldn't figure out quite how the conversation got to that point. I glanced at Dan, who hadn't stopped laughing, and knew it was too late and I was committed to my answer. I nodded again, this time with a bit more hesitation because I now knew what exactly I was agreeing to. "Uh, yup. Sure." I didn't even know parrots liked melons, but I guess that detail was unimportant considering the big picture of the question.

Bill scoffed at me in disgust again and leaned back farther away from me. "Ya got some strange desires there, Benny," he said. Dan continued to laugh, and Sweet Gary tried his best to hide a chuckle behind a rather choking cough. I just nodded and stared at Dan, patiently waiting for him to cease his laughter and give me the letters. Dan finally began to calm down, taking deep breaths to get air back into his lungs.

"Oh, Ben, man, that was great!" Dan said in between gasps. "Here, take the fuckin' things so ya can stop dazin' off about 'em!" He stretched his hand holding the letters out toward me.

I ripped the envelopes out of his awaiting hand with frustration and quickly looked to see whom they were addressed to. One was addressed to me; the other to John. Both were in Mrs. Cummings's beautiful handwriting, and upon seeing both of our names so casually drawn out in her scrawl, a lump quickly formed in my throat and made it difficult for me to swallow. For some reason, I suddenly felt guilty while opening her letter. I could feel the guys watching me expectantly, waiting for me to open it and hoping that I might divulge details about its contents. I took a deep breath and slid my index finger beneath the envelope's glued-down flap. My finger began to lift up, and I felt the brief restraint of the glue before it gave away beneath my finger. I slowly exhaled, the shaky air escaping through my teeth with a quiet whistle. When my breath had left me completely, I pulled my finger back and stared at the half-opened envelope.

"I ... uh ... I'm gonna go to the tent," I said, quickly standing up from the wooden bench. I kept my eyes trained on the letter in my hands, biting my lip with curiosity and concern at what contents it might hold. I heard the guys saying "Sure" and "So long" as I walked away, but I couldn't bring myself to acknowledge them. I threw back the entry flap of the tent I now shared with Gary, and flung myself on the previously unoccupied spare cot. I stared at the letter addressed to me, flipping it over and over in my hands. A part of me contemplated never opening it, letting it keep all its secrets and whispered idolatries. As it was, unopened, it remained untainted by betrayal and the reality that had engulfed the situation outside its precious paper barrier. I lay there contemplating this and many other silly and rather pathetic notions before I gave up and knew that no matter how special this last letter may seem, no matter how much I wanted to preserve it, my curiosity would always get the better of me. With that final acknowledgment, I tore the rest of the flap open and gently slid the folded letter from its paper haven. My dark eyes began to skim the swirling words, eager to drink in what Mrs. Cummings had to say.

After I read the entirety of the letter once, I reread it—slower this time, so as not to miss any details. I began to chew on my lip, a nervous habit that I was developing because of all the stress from the past week. If I'd had cigarettes, I would have taken up smoking, but being on an island in the middle of fucking nowhere made it difficult to start expensive habits. I closed my eyes and pinched the bridge of my nose. After reading Mrs. Cummings's latest news, I couldn't let John read his letter alone. It didn't matter that he hated me, or that he wanted nothing to do with me or anyone for that matter. I reread her letter two or three more times, making sure that it was indeed there in oily black and yellowed white: "fatal accident."

◆ ◆ ◆

I waited inside John's tent for a couple of hours, just sitting on my former cot, staring up at the tiny holes in the canvas and trying to form constellations out of them. I had his letter resting on my chest, looking so innocent in its white disguise, giving no indication of what dreadful news lurked within it.

It was past dark and I was about to give up and go back to my own tent when he walked in. At first he didn't notice me and sat down on his bed, letting out a heavy sigh. With that one sigh his shoulders slumped and fell from their noble posture to a more humbled and burdened one. He brought his hands up and roughly entwined them in his blond hair, a deep grumble coming from his throat. He took in a few deep breaths and exhaled sharply before pushing himself up and walking toward his trunk to undress for bed. I watched him silently as he did all this, not wanting to interrupt his relaxation.

I was also, on a more selfish level, entranced as I watched his behavior. Only a few times had I ever seen him lay down his sword and shield, remove his armor, and allow himself to feel the world around him. Each time I witnessed it, I couldn't help but be mesmerized. When he lay down his shield and just existed with the world, he seemed very human. That energy of his engulfed others, who were able to glimpse briefly the complexity of his character. Most of the time he was straitlaced, quiet, and clam with a short fuse if you pushed the right buttons; everything else just rolled off his shoulders, and he would smile, making his eyes twinkle intimidatingly. But beneath it all, beyond the cornflower blue and that unique energy, was a vulnerability that heard and felt everything.

He was in the middle of slowly unbuttoning his shirt, his long fingers making the task look painful, when he noticed me lying on my old bed. He paused briefly in his actions, his shoulders quickly rising and his spine straightening to give no indication that he had ever let them fall. "What are you doing here?" he asked gruffly, slipping his shirt off and folding it to place it in his trunk for another day.

I watched him a moment longer, trying to figure out how I should introduce the letter. I had been lying there for at least two hours, and yet I still hadn't found a good way to do it. Just as there is no good way to say, "I'm in love with your mom," you'd be hard pressed to find a nice way to say, "You found out I fucked your mom, but she wrote us both letters and I already read mine and there's a nasty surprise waiting for you in it. Enjoy!" Yeah, I really sucked at this kind of shit. I blame my parents; they should've trained me how to handle delicate situations in my upbringing.

I swung my legs over the side of the bed and sat up. The letter fell casually off my chest and into my lap, catching John's attention. I picked up the letter and held it out to him. "You got a letter from your mom today," I said flatly.

John didn't move. He remained perfectly still and just stared at the letter as if it might bite him if he reached for it. His jaw clenched, and I could tell he was debating whether or not to take it. Finally, he turned back to his trunk and closed the lid so that he could prop his foot on it while he untied the laces of his boots.

"I don't want it," he said, slipping the boot and sock off of one foot and propping the other on the trunk to unlace it. I kept my arm outstretched and pushed myself off of the bed. I took one step closer to him and firmly held the letter by his face. John lifted his head to glare at me while he slipped his other boot and sock off.

"You really need to read this letter," I said, my voice still flat and void of any joking or lightheartedness. I didn't want to risk John rejecting the letter again because he thought I wasn't serious. I saw some surprise drift across his face because of my tone; he no doubt recognized the rarity of me being completely serious. This didn't happen very often, and let's face it, I hated it, but there was no way he could afford not to believe me. He looked back at the letter in my hand, the corner of the yellowed paper gently scraping across his cheek whenever he moved. He looked briefly back at my still serious face and, with great trepidation, finally lifted his hand up and took hold of the letter. After I checked to be sure that the letter was firmly in his grasp, I took a few steps back and waited for him to open it and learn of the news I had read about two hours earlier. He flipped the envelope over and tore the flap open to reveal a trifold piece of paper. John glanced up at me with hesitation, his fingers hovering over the letter. I nodded at him, urging him to continue, before spinning around to give him some privacy while he read her letter.

I stared at the canvas of the tent for a few minutes before finding myself fidgety, waiting for his reaction. I bent down and gently fingered the linen of the sheets on my old cot, noting that sand had found its way into its previously undisturbed creases. Seems the damn stuff was attempting to replace me already. No respect, that fucking sand. After what felt like an eternity (but was, in all honesty, only about a minute or two—if that), my body was literally itching to turn around and speak to John about what had happened back home. I tried to resist it, scratching at the itch in my torso, but alas, my curiosity got the best of me, as it always does. I spun around, my hand involuntarily going to my own letter from Mrs. Cummings, which I had stuffed in my pocket, and tried to read John's face. His brow was furrowed deeply over his eyes, and his hand was cradling his chin inquisitively. His eyes scanned over the letter again and again, but his face never displayed any definitive emotion.

"I ... uh ... I'm sorry, man," I said lamely. I reached my hand up behind my head and awkwardly scratched my hair, noticing how long it had gotten since we arrived. John just nodded his head absently. I waited a little longer, mentally trying to urge him to look up at me and say something.

Eventually John let out a heavy sigh and let both of his hands drop to his sides. With that sigh, his shoulders slumped forward and the lines on his face transformed his expression from one of confusion to one of complete weariness. I took a step toward him but stopped when he lifted his head up and looked at me. His eyes were filled with an intense sadness I hadn't expected to see, and they were heavy with regret.

"So ... he ... uh ... he's dead," he said, choking his words out slowly. I nodded silently and waited for him to continue. "I take it you got a letter explaining the whole thing too?" he asked. He cleared his throat with discomfort, and once again I nodded. He slapped the letter against his leg absentmindedly while his other hand gently massaged the back of his neck. His eyes stared off into space, contemplating god knows what about the whole situation. I licked my lips and glanced down at my feet, which were shifting under my weight uncomfortably. I blame my parents for not teaching me how to deal with these kinds of situations. I really do.

"So, how … what are you feeling?" I asked nervously. When John didn't say anything right away, I was certain that he didn't want me there, but no matter how much I tried to convince my feet to turn and leave, the damn things refused to budge. So I waited. I waited so long in that stretched-out silence that the silence itself began to have a sound.

"I can't believe he's gone. I … I just can't believe that it's over," John whispered. He stiffly made his legs move, one small shuffling step at a time, until he collapsed on his cot in a solemn heap. He was nearly bent in half, the weight of his shoulders pressing him down upon his thighs and into the mattress. I sat down across from him on my cot and folded my hands in my lap.

"It … it just seems so anticlimactic, you know? I mean, after all this time, the Dragon is finally slain and … and …" He trailed off hopelessly, his eyes once again staring off into the space between us.

"And it wasn't you that slayed him," I said.

John's eyes snapped to mine, and he stared at me for a minute before nodding in affirmation. I took in a deep breath and slowly let it out. All these years, all of his attempts, and it wasn't him that brought the Dragon down. There was a deep sadness emanating from John, enveloping me like that energy of his usually did and pressing heavily upon my heart. I couldn't tell what upset him more—that his father was dead, or that he hadn't been the one to defeat him.

"Well, you've got to be proud of her at least," I said, hoping that it would pull him out of the devouring depression that was settling upon him.

His eyes became quizzical, and his brow furrowed deeply once more. "Proud of who?" he asked, somewhat bitingly. I let out a curt laugh of disbelief before responding:

"Your mom, of course!" I said with a chuckle, wondering how he had passed over that part of the letter. My chuckles ceased, however, when I noticed he was still just as puzzled as before.

He gave a small shrug, lifting one heavy shoulder before letting it drop. "I guess it seems like she's handling it pretty well. I suppose I'm proud of her for that," he muttered, sinking further into the mattress.

I opened my mouth to speak again, to ask him how he could have missed the most important part of her letter, when I realized that the letter he held in his hand was not like the letter folded up in my pocket.

"May ... may I see your letter?" I asked, my hand reaching out for the piece of paper. I noticed that John's eyes became icy at my request—clearly indicating that he had not forgotten our previous argument and I wasn't anywhere near to being off the hook—but he thrust it roughly at me anyway. I nodded my thanks and began to read his single-page letter. I skipped over the part where she told him how Red had finished up her schooling and was going to be making a trip to Kansas to look for a job so she could help out during this "horrific war." All that had been the same in my letter, except that Mrs. Cummings was a little more forthcoming about why Red was really moving back; she also told me she was trying to convince the poor girl that if she wrote John a letter explaining her plans to him, he would be "most pleasantly surprised and joyful." For John's sake I hoped she would, but I digress. Eventually I got to the part where Mrs. Cummings explained the Dragon's death, and I was shocked by the amount of detail that she had provided me but not him.

I'm so sorry to have to tell you through a letter, Johnny, but your father has passed. The sheriff declared that it was an accident. He said that your father must've been intoxicated, and in his drunken stumbling he fell on the upturned prongs of the pitchfork I had borrowed from the Millers to clear out my garden. Since you left, it's been overrun by weeds and groundcover. The Millers and the Halperts have both offered for me to stay with them while the funeral is being prepared. It's a sweet offer, but I don't expect the whole thing to take too long.

We both know no one will show up anyway. I love you, and I miss you terribly. Come home safely to me.

> *Love always,*
> *Your mother*

I stared at the inked words curling on the page for a while, my brain trying to comprehend why our two letters would be so different. Why wouldn't she want John to know the truth? Maybe she just had no easy way to tell him; maybe she was trying to protect him. I looked up from the letter at John's defeated posture, and for the first time since Mrs. Cummings and I began our relationship, I knew that he couldn't be sheltered from her secrets anymore. I couldn't bear to see another weight added to his shoulders, especially since I knew that one day it could be the very thing that would break him.

"John," I said, pulling out my crumpled letter. John raised his head from where it had been resting against his chest and looked at me patiently, silently. I stretched out my arm and held my letter from Mrs. Cummings out to him. He quickly frowned, and he looked repeatedly from the letter to my face. "I think you need to read my letter too."

John shook his head and shoved my outstretched hand away from him. "No, I've had my fill of reading your letters," he said sharply.

I winced and pulled the letter away from him. He'd never told me just how many of my letters he had read. I often wondered, during that week that we weren't speaking, how he managed to push himself to read so many unchaste words from his own mother, but I figured out that the only reason he would have suffered through so many intimate letters from her would be to comprehend the fullest extent of my deepest betrayal. I couldn't help but chuckle humorlessly as I stared at the papers in my hand that represented to him just how horribly stupid I could be. "Yeah, you certainly have, haven't you?"

John glared coolly at me, but his eyes no longer held the betrayal that they had a week before. I took that to be a promising sign that he was slowly forgiving me. That's not to say I wouldn't have some extensive groveling to do before he'd ever trust me again, but I thought perhaps this could be the start.

"I'll read it to you then. You have to know what she told me that she didn't tell you. It'll help you understand things that I just … maybe if you hear her words in this letter you'd get it." I paused before opening the letter, waiting for John to yell and scream about not wanting to hear his mother write me sweet nothings or to break my nose or just pull out a knife and slit my throat—there were a lot of different reactions to this that I was attempting to prepare myself for. Luckily, he didn't do any of those things.

He simply flopped backward on his cot so he was half lying, half sitting. He folded his hands across his bare belly while his legs draped over the frame of the cot and he just lay there, silently and patiently waiting for me to proceed, without any more objections or protests. Taking that as my cue, I began to read. I skipped the beginning, where she told me all about Red and how much she still loved John. I skipped over the part where she told me she missed me and my idiotic jokes because I always managed to make her smile—even if I was being stupid. I skipped over everything John didn't need to hear until I got to the part that he did need to hear.

"'I do have a rather unpleasant reason for writing you this time. My husband had a fatal accident and has passed away. Your father and the sheriff came by and decided that he must've been intoxicated and had drunkenly stumbled upon the pitchfork I had borrowed from the Millers to clear out my garden that you boys planted for me all those years ago. Since you and John left I haven't been able to keep up with it, so it got overrun by groundcover and weeds. Accidents happen, I guess. But then again, I already told you that a long time ago. Truth is I had decided now would be a good time to fix up my garden because I was sick of the way things were, and I wanted to see some new growth.'"

I paused and glanced up at John to make sure he was listening. He hadn't moved from his reclined position on the bed, but I could tell he was paying attention by how tense his forearms had suddenly become and how his hands had moved from their resting place on his bare stomach to his thighs, where his fingers were slowly starting to grip the fabric of his pants.

"I don't get how I had to hear this, Ben. It doesn't seem any different from what was in my letter," he said, but still he didn't sit up. I nodded, even though I knew he couldn't see me, and continued.

"I haven't got to that part yet—"

"Then get there," he said briskly. He was losing patience and was getting cranky, no doubt due to the hour and whatever was going on in that skull of his.

"All right. 'Since you both left, I've been on my own with that man. I've never been alone with just him and me; you and John always provided plenty of distractions. I'm so proud of you both for joining the Marines and fighting for our nation, and if you boys had never left, I don't know how long it would've taken me to reach my breaking point. Ben, I just couldn't take it anymore. My husband is gone, and despite how much I may hope and wish and pray, he will never come back.

'I didn't want to correct your father or the sheriff with their hypothesis; it just seems like it's best for everyone if things are left the way they are, but I needed to tell you, Ben. You're the only one that will understand; you're the only one that understands all of me. He wasn't drunk at all when it happened. I told the sheriff that I was in the house when it happened, but I was actually outside in the garden at the time. We had had a nice conversation—the first in many years, and tragically the last as well. He was hungover, but with the haze of alcohol gone from his bloodshot eyes I could actually see traces of the man he once was. He told me that he was sorry for how the past few years had been. I think John's departure awakened him to what life had become, and underneath all the whiskey, he hated the way things were. He said he was going to try and turn things around, try to be better and get a job and go back to the way it used to be.

'For a brief moment, Ben, I believed him. Then I saw the keys to the truck in his hand, and I knew that you and John were right. My husband was gone and never coming back, and all that came out of this man's mouth now were lies. At least I have the comfort knowing that the last thing I said to my husband was that I loved him, and for that second just before it happened, I saw his old self in those eyes and knew that he loved me too. But then it was all over, and he was impaled on the pitchfork. As I told you before, accidents happen.'"

I stopped reading and looked up from the letter to observe John's reaction. He hadn't moved at all during my narration. He hadn't even twitched. Even after my final words hung in the air he remained still, his hands clenched in the fabric of his pants and his bare chest gently rising and falling with his steady breathing. I briefly wondered if the ass bag had fallen asleep on me, but when I stood up to check, his eyes were still wide open and looking contemplatively around the tent.

"John?" I said, standing over his reclined form.

He continued to stare straight up at the roof of the tent and refused to look at me. Eventually his hands released their hold on his pants and he once again brought them to rest on his belly.

"Thank you for bringing me my letter, Ben," he whispered dismissively.

Disappointed that this was how he was going to react (even though I wasn't too surprised; he never was one for talking in the moment—that was always what I did), I nodded my head and turned to make my way back to my new tent with Sweet Gary.

"Ben?" he called after me when I reached the flap of the tent.

Confused, I turned back to see that he still hadn't even sat up. "Yeah?"

"Leave your letter," he said softly.

I felt my lips twisting into the first genuine smile I've managed since our brawl as I put my letter on his cot beside his head and left. He might need a few more days to himself, but he was starting to understand what I was too stupid to be able to communicate: that his mother was so much more than what she'd shown him. Mrs. Cummings was a very strong and proud woman, and I hoped that, through my letter, John would be able to see that. John hadn't gotten to slay the Dragon, but I had no doubt that Mrs. Cummings had.

October 1935

I closed my eyes as the warm autumn breeze swept by my face, bringing the smell of crisp leaves and freshly turned soil with it. I inhaled deeply, taking the freshness in the air deep into my lungs. After the breeze passed, I slowly opened my eyes and tried not to squint in the bright afternoon sun. I smiled and looked over my shoulder at John to see if he was enjoying the fresh air as much as I was. It took some great persuading, and a few very misplaced and unsteady steps, but I eventually got John out of his room—away from his books and existential thoughts—and into the warm glow of the early October sun. His face was mostly expressionless as he stared at the edge of the woods that surrounded his house, watching the yellow and orange leaves lift off their branches and float down to the ground. We hadn't spoken since I had arrived and carried him outside, forbidding him to bring a book with him.

"Your mother told me that all you've been doing since you got outta the hospital is readin' and ignorin' the fuckin' world around you. So per her request, I am takin' you outside so you can get back in touch with this lovely world around us!" I had said to him enthusiastically, closing the tome in his hands and pushing him out of his bed. He hadn't been too happy about it, but once I got him outside and shoved him into the porch chair he stopped struggling and cursing and just sat there silently.

That was about an hour before, and he still hadn't said anything to me, but that wasn't too surprising. He'd been out of the hospital for one week and had hardly spoken in two. I'd been to see him every day he was in the hospital, trying to get him to smile and joke or punch me in the face or something, but he was rather closed off and unresponsive to everything. The only person that he had managed to summon a small reaction for was his mother. Whenever she came in the room, he would smile softly and indulge her with more than one word answers to her conversation attempts. I let out a contented sigh, listening to the sparrows in the trees sing and the leaves crunch as they fell onto piles of their brothers that had let go before them. I set the rake in my hands down on the ground and strode out of Mrs. Cummings's garden and up to the porch, where John was sitting morosely.

"It's a nice day, ain't it Johnny?" I asked, plopping into the chair next to him, taking another deep breath in and smiling.

John just ignored me and continued to stare at the trees as they tenderly swayed in the breeze. "Hey, Ben?" he finally said, his deep voice raspy from lack of use. Surprised that John had actually begun a conversation, I quickly turned to look at him.

"Yeah, John?" I asked. He still hadn't moved his gaze from the colorful trees ahead of us, but his head turned ever so slightly toward me.

"I was thinking. I know there's probably a lot of talk going around town about what happened, but I'd like to keep the details between just us," he said. Toward the end of his sentence, his eyes drifted from the swaying trees to stare seriously at me.

I nodded my head slowly. This was the first time since the encounter with the Dragon that he'd mentioned it at all. I'd tried to bring it up a couple of times while he was in the hospital, but he had simply remained silent and turned away from me, signaling the end of the conversation. "All right," I said. "What are you gonna tell people instead?" I wanted to make sure that we were on the same page and that I wouldn't fuck up by disclosing information he didn't want me to disclose.

He lowered his eyes for a moment, bringing his hand up to rest on his chin as he contemplated his response to my question. "Well, I don't know. I guess we can just make shit up on an as-needed basis."

I shrugged and nodded. "Sure. Okay."

Silence filled in between us, and we both turned our attention back to the beautiful afternoon that surrounded us.

"Hey, Ben?" John said again.

I tossed my head back and slowly leaned it against the back of the chair, flopping it to the side so that I could look at John lazily. "Hmm?"

John twisted completely in his chair to face me this time. "Thanks for coming with me into the Dragon's lair and for, you know … Especially since I had been such a jerk right before, what with me punching you and all." He cleared his throat uncomfortably and lowered his eyes shamefully to his hand, which was nervously picking at the wooden armrest.

I smiled and flipped my head back so that I was no longer looking at John and was once again staring at the garden I had been tending for him. "Of course, man. Where would a knight be without his squire, right?" I said.

I heard John softly chuckle and resituate himself in his chair. "Yeah, where would I be?"

November 1941

Once I got back to my new tent, Gary was already asleep and snoring softly. I had thought about trying to write more of my letter to Mrs. Cummings but decided against it. After reading her letters to me and to John, I had so much more I wanted to say, but my brain refused to convert those thoughts into something tangible. I quietly undressed, folded my shirt and pants to wear the next day, and crawled into bed. I lay there many hours, unmoving, listening to the turning of the tide and Gary's gentle breathing, trying desperately to remember the smell of newly turned soil and the freshness of an autumn wind.

◆ ◆ ◆

Dawn came all too soon. Gary was always very cheerful in the morning, chatting and smiling while he got ready, and it made me respect and long for John's steady quietness. During breakfast I briefly contemplated paying attention to the conversation between the boys before I gave up and settled into my own thoughts. I couldn't help but think about what Mrs. Cummings had talked about in her letter or, more importantly, what she had ended her letter with. If I had still had it, I would have taken it out and stared contemplatively at it for long periods of time, trying not to allow myself to hope too much. For the most part the boys just let me be, for which I was grateful. I had heard Gary whisper to Dan that I hadn't slept much the night before, and I knew that based on that, and combined with the letters, Dan could infer that I wasn't in much of a joking mood that morning.

I had been drifting in and out of my thoughts when a sudden silence surrounded us that shocked me to attention. I looked up at the guys and noticed that they were all staring at something behind me. I gauged their faces to figure out whether I needed to be concerned or not, but their expressions confused me even more. Bill was simply nodding his head in approval, Dan had a small smile curling at the corners of his lips, and Sweet Gary was just all-out grinning like a schoolboy. Before I could turn around to take a look for myself, I felt the empty bench to my left shake under the weight of someone sitting down.

"Morning, guys! What've I missed?" John asked smoothly, looking each man in the face with a polite smile on his lips. Gone was the depressing air about him and the cold from his eyes. The man that now sat beside me was the John that used to sit beside me every morning; his vibrant and addicting energy had returned to engulf us. I smiled at him and slowly began to eat my now cold breakfast that had been lying untouched on my tray.

"Well, buddy, you've missed quite a bit since you've been off frolickin' with Jim and his womanly section!" Bill said, leaning forward excitedly. John's smile widened, and he listened attentively as Bill and Gary dove into the series of stories they had recounted the night before. I glanced over at John once during the meal, taking it all in. He seemed just as he had before, as if the past week and a half had been nothing more than a dream. He was laughing and joking and indulging the men by participating in their hypotheticals. Despite all that, there was an undeniable change as well. His shoulders seemed a little lighter, as if a massive weight had been lifted, and his chest puffed out with more genuine confidence than I'd seen in a very long time.

"It's a damn good thing our section is back together now," Dan said, changing the topic from ridiculous stories and questions.

Bill nodded strongly with agreement and certainty. "Yup. They're bringin' in some navy commander in a couple of days." Gary furrowed his brow in confusion and looked toward John to see if he had heard of this information.

"Really? Who is it?" John asked, apparently just as in the dark as Gary and I. Gary leaned across the table and whispered to me: "How is it those two always get all the information first?"

I laughed and shook my head, bringing up my hand and gently shoving Sweet Gary back onto his bench. "Beats me, kid. I've learned to just accept it and be thankful someone here knows what the hell is goin' on out there." Gary laughed and turned back to hear Dan's answer.

"Commander Cunningham, or something like that. He's a navy officer but he's gonna be headin' up operations down here and conducting inspections on all units as soon as he arrives," said Dan. We continued the conversation, speculating on the reasons as to why we were getting a navy commander of all people, just how much of a hard-ass he was going to be, and if we'd be able to meet his expectations, which were rumored to be pretty high.

I glanced back at John and reflected on the changes between us. There was still a space between us, an uncertainty that neither one of us knew what to do with, but it was this space that we could once again grow into. I turned away from John and looked at the laughing men in front of us. Back to the way things were before or not, it would still be another two weeks before John would be willing to talk about it. Until then I just followed his lead (as I always did, because I was an amazing squire like that) and continued to ponder Mrs. Cummings' closing words: "With my husband gone there are so many new possibilities including all of the ones I had never allowed myself to hope for before."

December 1, 1941

"Have you finished that thing yet?" John asked when he walked into our tent. I signed my name at the bottom of my letter to Mrs. Cummings and stuffed it into its envelope.

"Yeah, just finished." I licked the adhesive around the edges and sealed the envelope.

"'Bout time. It's taken you nearly three weeks to write the damn thing," John said lightly as he flopped down on my cot beside me. I nodded my head and stared at the rather bulky envelope in my hands. I could hardly believe that I had actually finished the letter, because every time I thought I had over the past three weeks, I always found something else I wanted to add and something else I wanted to say. I felt horrible telling Mrs. Cummings everything through a letter, but given the current geographical separation, I didn't really have much of a choice. John sat beside me silently while I twirled the envelope edge over edge in my fingers. I heaved a deep sigh, flipped it so that it was face forward, and addressed the damn thing. John patted my knee encouragingly and watched me stand up and place it on my shirt so I would remember to mail it the next day.

"Thank you, Ben," he whispered. I nodded and returned to my spot beside him. About a week after John had learned of his father's demise and returned to our section, he told me that I could come back to our tent. Now, he didn't go and say it like that; we weren't some old married couple having a disagreement (no matter what Dan might say.) He simply stated that the sand was starting to pile up on my cot and I should get in there and clean it off because it was starting to really piss him off. So to appease him (and for my own selfish battle against the sand) I thanked Gary for helping me out and moved back to my old tent and showed that fucking sand what was what. Once I moved back in to my original location, it didn't take too much time for John to resume his old ways. There was still that space between us: that thing we hadn't talked about yet. I knew it wouldn't be too much longer until John was ready to discuss the Dragon and his mother. Until he was, though, I was just going to wait and continue bullshitting as I always did.

"I'm going to go for a quick walk," I said to John, my eyes staring at the letter. A part of me wanted to reach out and rip it all up, but I knew that I couldn't do that.

John turned his head to the side to eye me over his shoulder while he continued to do his nightly procedures for turning in. "All right," he said.

I nodded thankfully and bolted from the tent. The air felt significantly cooler at night than it did during the day, even though I knew the temperature barely dropped. I took a deep breath in and walked toward the beach, stopping on my way to let the guards know that I was there so that they wouldn't accidently shoot me or anything. The guys that had duty overnight had gotten accustomed to seeing me there most nights since the fight. "No problem, man," said one of the guards—Adam, I think. "But you don't have very long: five minutes at best."

I nodded and thanked him, letting him know that I wouldn't stay past my curfew. I meandered along the beach, hating each individual grain of sand that found its way into my boots, until I came to a rock that I could sit on. I lowered myself onto the cold, rough surface and tilted my head toward my stars. If there was one thing I enjoyed about this fucking island, it was that there was nothing to block the stars from me. I had never seen so many stars unobscured by the lights of the town or the trees out by my and John's houses. I sat there for a few minutes, picking out my favorite heroes and recounting their tales in my mind. I had tried for years to teach John about the stars, but he always drifted off somewhere and lost interest. He'd never come out and say he wasn't interested, though. He knew that after shoving so many literary "masterpieces" down my throat for our whole lives, he owed me this. I could tell when he stopped listening, though. He would get very quiet, his eyes would be fixed on only one spot in the sky, and I would know I had lost him to the inner workings of his brain.

I didn't care though; I would still ramble on about how they were light-years away and how a light-years is a measurement of distance and not time despite what it sounds like. I would explain that each star was a burning ball of gas and that though many of them were no longer burning, they still appeared to be burning to us because it took so long for their light to reach our sky. He would just make noises of agreement and oohs and ahhs when appropriate. I would go on and on about the science, about how stars burned blue, yellow, and red based on their level of heat, and I knew that he heard none of it. If I ever wanted to bring him back, if I wanted to snap him out of his little world, all I would have to do is point out my heroes and tell him their myths. John always loved a good story.

April 1941

John was working late, and Mrs. Cummings and I were far across town on an isolated hill in the middle of barren fields. I gently brushed the soft curls off of Mrs. Cummings's forehead, my calloused fingers brushing the smooth span of her porcelain forehead. Her perfect lips curved slightly into an innocent smile of contentment as her deep blue eyes followed my finger, which was pointed toward the heavens. She snuggled closer to my chest, where her head was resting, pushing her breasts and stomach into my side and draping her leg across mine, which were stretched out comfortably in the grass. My arm was wrapped around her, and my hand continued to brush her hair tenderly while I pointed out my favorite constellations.

"That one is Hydra. It's named after the sea serpent and is the largest constellation in the sky. See, it runs from the head here to the tail down there." I illustrated by following the curve of the serpent with my finger.

Mrs. Cummings smiled and nodded encouragingly. "I see it," she whispered sweetly, her fingers gently tracing soft circles on my stomach.

I smiled down at her before turning my head back to the sky. "It was one of the beasts that Hercules had to defeat in his twelve labors for the king. This was a beast with nine snake heads. Each time Hercules cut one of the heads off, two more would grow back in its place." I felt her shiver against me, but she never commented on the chill.

"So how'd he beat it?" she asked imploringly.

I smiled and turned toward her, my warm breath caressing her cheek when I spoke. "To defeat the Hydra, Hercules ran around cutting off all the heads while his charioteer sealed the wounds with a torch so that they couldn't grow back." I said.

Mrs. Cummings shivered in my arms again and continued to stare at the sky. "What's a charioteer?" She asked. I gave a shrug and snuggled closer to her.

"It's a lot like a squire—but for the ancient Greeks." I said with a chuckle. She turned and looked at me, brushing my face for a moment with her long fingers.

"So the squire is the one who really saved the day?" She asked, teasingly. I shook my head and kissed her palm.

"Nah, it was a joint effort. Hercules couldn't have done it without his charioteer, and the charioteer couldn't have done it without the hero." I said, smiling at her. Warmth filled me as she giggled, kissed my cheek, and turned back to the sky. I turned my head away from her and searched for another constellation.

"There! That's Leo, the lion. Not only is he part of the zodiac, but he was the first of Hercules's twelve labors. Apparently he had a hide that couldn't be pierced by iron, bronze, or stone. Hercules needed his pelt for the king, so Hercules strangled him."

Mrs. Cummings gasped beside me and watched my finger as it traced the noble lion. "That's awful!" she exclaimed softly. I chuckled and brought my arm down so it could wrap around her and pull her closer to me. I looked down at her and found her blue eyes staring affectionately into mine.

"Leo was also worshiped by the Egyptians. They believed that he marked the spot where the sun rose after creation, and they associated his appearance in the night sky with the flooding of the Nile, that which brought good fortune and food. So don't worry; Hercules may have killed him, but he was still idolized."

She smiled and brought her head up to meet my lips and kissed me. Her lips were cold at first but rapidly warmed up with the passion of our kiss. We broke apart, taking in deep, calming breaths of cool night air.

"You're very smart, Ben; I don't understand how you failed so many of your classes," she said teasingly.

I laughed and smiled mischievously at her. "Now don't go givin' me credit where I don't deserve it. The only reason I know all of this is because I like readin' about it. I read all the books John made me read, but I didn't once open one for school. I guess I'm just too lazy." I brushed a fallen blonde curl out of her eyes. Mrs. Cummings laughed sweetly and kissed me again.

"Too lazy and too stubborn," she said. I nodded, my lips parted in a goofy grin. I kissed her again and we lay there in the cool grass, the stars spread out over us like a protective bubble sheltering us from the rest of the world.

"Ben," she whispered, pulling back a little to look into my eyes. I smiled gently at her, my hand rubbing her back, pulling the fabric of her shirt out of her skirt a little at a time until I could finally feel her skin. I felt her shiver a little at my touch, but she continued to speak. "I'm really proud of you for joining the Marines." She leaned back into me and brought her frozen hand up to cup my face. "But how I wish you weren't going."

My hand stalled on her back, and my free arm lifted to my face and grabbed her hand. I pulled it away from my face and kissed her knuckles, my lips leaving bursts of warmth on her skin. "Me too," I whispered, and I kissed her deeply.

December 1, 1941

"Gotta head out, Ben," Adam said, awakening me from my reverie. I nodded and forced a smile. I took one last look at the stars and the sea that together stretched out forever, seeming to meet in eternity before falling off the side of the world and into an abyss. Wake Island really was the most isolated place on Earth. I walked back to my tent and ignored John as I undressed and climbed onto my cot. I pulled up the blanket and rolled over. It was still warm on the island, but after staring at my stars for so long, I felt a chill crawl through me that just wouldn't go away. I closed my eyes knowing that in the morning I would mail the letter for John. All that I would have left of Mrs. Cummings would be my memories of our impenetrable world beneath those stars.

December 3, 1941

Tensions among the men were getting higher. I don't just mean between Dan, Bill, and Gary; I mean tensions among all the men on our little bar of sand were climbing. Fights were breaking out a little more frequently, and since the new commander arrived, our duties had been ratcheted up a notch. Luckily I hadn't been a part of any brawls since the night we all confronted Jim and his section. That's not to say that it wouldn't have happened; we all know what a dumbass I could be. But Jim had been steering clear of us. Thank god for that! I guess the guy did have some brains that weren't shit in that head of his.

To be honest, I caught myself wondering sometimes what's made him stay away. Sometimes I thought it was guilt ... but that would mean Jim wasn't a completely self-centered douchefuck and that he actually had a heart in his chest cavity somewhere. I quickly ruled that out as an option and chalked it up to the fact that none of us wanted Captain Michaels to get Major Devereux—or worse, the navy commander—involved.

Bill heaved a heavy sigh as he slumped onto the bench beside me. "Lord, I'm beat!" he said. I turned and looked at him dully, sympathy completely lacking on my face. Dan plopped down on the opposite bench, looking equally exhausted and staring blankly at the natural pattern in the wooden table.

"No shit," I said. "We all are. We've been bustin' our asses to get everythin' up to Cunningham's standards for the past week." Bill nodded without looking at me and just slumped deeper into himself until he was resting his head on his meaty arms on the table.

"Well I think it's great!" John said enthusiastically, climbing in beside me.

Bill lifted his head up and stared at John in disgust. "What the hell's got ya still chirpy?" he asked. I shook my head and leaned into my hand that was propped up by my elbow on the table. Bill sure wasn't the sharpest tool in the box, because he had just given John a reason to unleash an awe-inspiring lecture that would move us, no doubt, to boredom.

"I just think it's fantastic that Commander Cunningham is upping the standards so that we can get this airstrip and everything completed faster in preparation for an attack! Just think of it. We could be hit at any moment, and you've noticed that everyone's getting a little antsier these days. Commander Cunningham is handling the situation right! The more prepared we are, the better the men will feel. Not only are they contributing, which is allowing them distractions from the thought of imminent battle, but they are also getting peace of mind that when it happens, we will be prepared!"

Bill stared blankly at him as he continued his zealous speech, going on and on about philosophies of the masses and some shit about "mob mentality" and how a working man is a man at peace. The whole thing reeked of bullshit to me, so I stopped listening. A small part of me wanted to turn to him and remind him about how I had fucked his mother just to shut him up. I was dumb, but unfortunately, I wasn't that dumb so I had to let him just keep talking.

"I agree completely!" said Gary. "I feel better myself having more to do each day." He began leaning in toward John. I stared dully at the two of them for a moment, my brain refusing to let any more of their conversation sink in. I looked over at Bill, who had managed to burrow his head deeper into his pillowed arms. Serves him right for unleashing this upon us all, I thought. It was bad enough when it was just John lecturing or motivating, but now he had somehow brainwashed Sweet Gary into joining him, the brilliant sick bastard. I slowly stood up from the bench, making sure to push Bill roughly out of my way.

"Watch it, Benjamina!" he said uncaringly. I just grunted in response and turned to John and Gary's bright, questioning faces. I glanced at Dan, who had his eyes half closed and his chin propped up in the palm of his hand, his head nodding gently in an attempt to keep from falling asleep.

"Where ya goin'?" Sweet Gary asked innocently.

I stared at him for a moment in contemplative silence before deciding not to insult the poor kid. "I'm just gonna turn in early. I don't really have it in me to be a star conversationalist tonight." John nodded sympathetically, and Bill released another groan but refused to move.

"All right, well see you in the mornin' then," Gary replied sweetly. I nodded absently and waved at them before turning around and heading toward my bunk.

"I think I'm gonna follow Ben's lead and turn in as well," I heard Dan's tired voice say from behind me. His departure was followed by a similar chorus of good-byes and another incomprehensible grunt from Bill. I paused briefly in my walking and waited for Dan to catch up to me.

"Bill's the biggest oaf I've met, givin' them twos a reason to go off like that," Dan said bitterly beside me. I nodded my agreement and continued to walk silently. Once we were a decent distance away from John and the others, I felt Dan lean in a little closer to me to ensure that our conversation remained private.

"So how're things with youse guys now?" he asked caringly.

I shrugged noncommittally and watched my boots sink into the sand with each step I took, allowing some of the tiny particles to pass through my laces and into my boot. Fucking sand. I knew Dan had wanted to ask about the status of our friendship, but he hadn't been able to find an opportune moment until now.

"It's better. He definitely loosened up about everythin' once I finally mailed that letter to Mrs. Cummings. We haven't talked any more about it yet, and I don't think we will for a while. John's the kind of guy that needs a lot of time to process his thoughts and all his options. He will go over every possible scenario to a conversation before he's even willin' to have it. He'll practically script the damn thing in his mind."

Dan nodded in understanding. Through all of this, he and I had actually gotten pretty close. I wasn't the kind of guy to go talking

151

about all my feelings and the like. I was not a woman, despite what Bill might claim, but I wasn't a closed book like John either. I didn't mind expressing my thoughts and observations and insight, but until Dan, no one really gave a damn to ask me for any of them—well, no one else except Mrs. Cummings, that is. John always assumed the role of the intellectual type, so people just assumed I was his dumb smartass squire that was too incompetent to have any thoughts worth any substance. I should be offended about being viewed and treated as such, but the truth is that there are very few people I actually care to engage with. I guess that's one reason I was such a smartass. I just didn't care about them, so I didn't really care to share my opinion; what difference would it make if I did?

"Have ya talked about his father yet?" Dan asked gently. I shook my head in response, and he nodded as if he had been expecting as much. We walked in a comfortable silence for a few paces before Dan turned to me, a mischievous glint in his eyes and a small smile on his lips that were already shadowed by the onslaught of a beard. "Ben, why is it you always refer to her as 'Mrs. Cummings'?" he asked.

I paused for a moment, pursing my lips in thought. My brow furrowed, and I searched my mind for an answer. It had never really occurred to me that I did this; it was just second nature, as much as calling John's girl "Red." I tilted my head to the right and shrugged. "I guess it just seemed disrespectful to call her anything else," I said.

Dan burst out with loud, uproarious laughter. I stared at him in confusion, which only seemed to fuel his rapture. "You're such a fuckin' idiot, Ben. God bless ya for it." He clapped me roughly on the back. I shook my head and waited for him to catch his breath before we continued toward our tents.

December 5, 1941

The days were starting to get shorter in terms of hours of sunlight, but we still worked from the darkness of the early morning to the darkness of night. It was a bit of a relief to no longer have the hot sun bearing down upon our bent backs as we worked, but it made it difficult to complete our assignments in the dark. We had heard rumors of peace between the Japanese and the Americans, but Commander Cunningham refused to let those rumors keep us from working like we had been to prepare ourselves for an attack. He reminded all the men that Wake Island was the last line of defense for America and that we had damn well better prove ourselves as Marines if it was necessary.

Consequently, the section had started to grow rather quiet since the arrival of the commander. Bill and Dan still cracked jokes and retold stories at Gary's request, but other than that, no one said much of anything. Part of this was because we were all starting to feel the same tension in our chests as the rest of the men, and no rumors of peace with the Japanese could unclench the fear of war that was slowly coiling itself around every man's heart. The other part was that this fear, this tension, was driving us all to work harder and faster, and none of us wanted to stop and really discuss why we felt the need to do so.

We were down by the coastal artillery guns doing our regular maintenance. Each day was getting so repetitive and it was starting to get to me. I looked up at Dan, who was working across from me, and noticed him talking quietly with John. Both of their faces were turned downward, so I couldn't make out the seriousness of the conversation, but based on how tense John's shoulders were and how his hands had paused in their twisting of a nut and bolt, I could infer. I frowned in confusion, searching my brain for any clues that might give away what Dan was telling him, but nothing came to mind. Whatever it was, the conversation didn't last long. I watched as Dan patted John on the back and walked away from him to grab another wrench. "Just think about it," I heard Dan say softly.

I watched Dan pick up his wrench and walk over to where Sweet Gary was working on gun number four and begin to help him. As Dan squatted down, his brown eyes looked up and met mine. There was a glaze of seriousness in them that was disappearing with each blink. He smiled warmly at me, refusing to admit anything about what had just transpired. I looked back to John and noticed that he had stood up, his back facing me, and was stretching out his long, sinewy arms. He turned around and smiled at me, but his smile didn't quite reach his eyes. I stared at him a moment longer before again bending down and getting back to work on the airstrip.

I glanced up and realized that John was still watching me contemplatively from the corner of his eye. I took a deep breath and let it out. Whatever Dan had said to him, it had removed the indifference that had filled John's eyes while he was in his thinking spell, and replaced it with an inquisitive curiosity that had never been there before. Whatever that meddling bastard had done, I suddenly got the feeling that he had sped up the waiting game and that John was now bursting with new questions and perspectives he had never thought of before. I glanced toward the darkening sky, which was streaked with warm yellows and pink. A doomed man always knows when it's coming. I looked at John before turning back to the sky and taking a sip of water, and I knew then that it was coming soon.

◆ ◆ ◆

All throughout dinner, John continued to stare at me with a confused and analytical expression on his face. I tried to ignore it, but it still gave me the willies and made me rather uncomfortable. It was as though I was a novel he had read three times before but had just now learned the language it was written in and it puzzled him. None of us wanted to waste much time talking to each other that night. Instead, we all decided to turn in early. I think the days were starting to get to us, and we couldn't really bullshit each other much longer; we were trying to disguise our wariness of the situation and failing horribly. Plus Dan and John were unsettling me with the way they kept looking at each other and then at me as if there were a secret conversation I was unknowingly a part of. It wasn't until we were back at the tent that I felt comfortable enough to confront John about it.

"What the hell is going on with you and Dan? It's freaking me out," I said. I was never much for beating around the bush when I wanted answers about something. I was far better at asking questions than answering them.

John looked shocked at my sudden outburst but laughed it off. "Sorry, Ben, Dan just got me thinking about something this afternoon is all. I didn't mean to freak you out." He chuckled again and continued to get ready for the night.

I narrowed my eyes at him in uncertainty. I didn't buy that as an answer for a second. I pursed my lips in contemplation and bit my tongue before deciding to go for it and just ask what I'd been wondering. "How're you handling the Dragon's death?" I asked finally.

John paused in the unbuttoning of his shirt. I crossed my arms uncomfortably, suddenly feeling like I pushed too soon and should've just waited until he initiated the conversation. It was too late now, and I wasn't about to back down. I was an idiot.

He shrugged and softly said, "I dunno, really. I don't feel like it's true. I still feel like, even though he's dead, I haven't beaten him yet."

I nodded and restrained myself from asking more follow-up questions. It was amazing that I even got that out of him. I turned from John and began to prepare myself for bed.

"Hey Ben, can I ask you something?" I heard John whisper behind me.

I shrugged off my shirt and nodded. "Sure. Go for it," I said. I was caught a little off guard by his question because he usually would just ask me anything with complete disregard as to whether or not I might be offended—mainly because I was rarely offended at anything. He paused before pushing onward, which made me a little wary, but I waited for him to speak all the same.

"Why my mother?" he asked.

I stiffened automatically, but when I saw that there was no anger in his eyes and no fury tightening his muscles, I relaxed a little. I paused a moment, debating how honest I should be, but after looking at the confused and needy cornflower-blue eyes that were staring imploringly into mine, I knew I just had to explain it fully. "Because, John, she actually listened to me and cared what I had to say. To her I wasn't just your squire or your stupid friend that followed you everywhere. To her I was simply Ben. No more, no less. There weren't any expectations; just understanding."

John didn't say anything. He nodded once and finished undressing. I watched him crawl into bed and turn away from me.

"G'night, Ben," he whispered sincerely. I finished undressing, swatted the sand off my cot, and lay there wondering what the hell Dan had said to him.

December 8, 1941

The morning of December 8 started much like any other, first with breakfast and then with our section heading to check the coastal artillery guns and do our daily inspection of them. Tensions had been rising over the past few months, and everyone seemed just a little more on edge than usual. Personally, I didn't really care. Sure, we were in a war, and yes, an attack could happen at any moment; but what would getting all uptight about the whole thing help? I couldn't change the situation, there was literally nothing more I could be doing to prepare, and since I signed up for the damn military in the first place, I couldn't really complain about it. That's not to say that there weren't moments in the early morning when the sun was just rising and the air was crisp with moisture when I blamed John for this whole mess.

Poor Gary, though, he was picking up on the other men's tensions, and I could see the boy getting jumpy. It was approaching 7:00 a.m., and we were just beginning our morning checks, but Gary was already far more tense than usual at that hour.

"Ya gotta calm down, boy!" Bill shouted, ducking under one of the guns to check the mechanics underneath it. Gary jumped a little at the booming of his deep voice, and I couldn't help but laugh.

John gave me a scolding look and clapped a soothing hand on young Gary's shoulders. "Ignore Ben, but Bill's right. You can't afford to be this worked up. If something does come our way, we need you calm and thinking clearly, or else you'll never be able to shoot one of these guns." I scoffed immaturely and proceeded with my checks.

Dan nodded and moved on to the next gun. "It's true," he said. "Besides, if somethin' was comin' our way, they'd alert us so that we could man our stations. We won't be unprepared. I guarantee ya, Gary." Dan smiled at Gary, and I could see the tension in the boy's shoulders ease and drop. Gary smiled back and nodded. I opened my mouth to say something that would undoubtedly make things worse and get my ass kicked by the rest of the guys, when every man on the island halted in his actions and listened to "General Quarters" as it sounded across the island. We looked at each other in shock, concern, and, in Gary's case, terror.

"What's that mean?" Gary asked.

I looked over toward Bill and Dan, who were scrambling to check all the guns to report and fix any malfunctions. John bent down and continued to do the same. Gary watched them all, panic rising in his face. I stood up, the fucking sand falling off my uniform as I walked toward him.

"Sweet Gary," I said, "that's the heads-up we told ya about. We gotta prepare for battle, 'cause it's headed this way." I patted his back more firmly than I had intended and dropped to my knees at the base of the last gun to inspect it. I tried my damnedest to keep my hands from shaking for Sweet Gary. Yup, there was nothing more I could do about it; I just had to pray that my training had been enough to prepare me for what was coming over the horizon. I guess the commander was right when he told us never to trust rumors of peace—especially during a war.

We scrambled to finish our work, and no man dared to speak in case it would throw off our concentration. At 8:50 they raised the flag, and we all stopped and stood at attention while Waronker played "To the Colors." I smiled to myself as I listened to the tune and noticed that he had played it perfectly. Once he finished, Bill let out a loud whoop, and his smile stretched widely across his face. "Didn't miss a beat that time, did he?" Bill said approvingly, his huge chest swelling with pride.

I chuckled and nodded.

"Not that time. You're quite right, Billy," John said. He patted Bill on the back and turned to go to his post. I stood there a moment longer, watching the stripes of our flag whip back and forth in the breeze.

"So this is it," Gary said, taking in a deep breath. I listened to Dan try to calm him without giving him false hope.

"Yup. Word is that they hit Pearl Harbor a few hours ago and are headin' this way. We'd better hurry up so that we're ready to take the bastards down." Dan pushed Gary in front of him, forcing his stiff legs to pick up the pace and get going. I quickly turned and followed them to our post. Our duty was to man the coastal artillery guns and defend our beaches from the invading enemy soldiers. It was five men to a gun: one to aim, one to fire, and three to load. The other guns had a sixth person to spot and relay coordinates, but our battery was short staffed which left our section without a spotter so Bill had to both check the coordinates that the major was sending us as well as line up the shot.

We each took our station and waited. Time seemed to slow while we listened to orders being shouted and sections of men and other batteries getting into position. I looked to my side, where John was positioned to help reload after I fired the weapon, and noticed that his face was that of the perfect soldier—the perfect knight. His brow was furrowed, and his eyes were bright and clear, sparkling with concentration. This is what he'd been waiting for: a time to prove that he was a stronger, better, and more honorable man than the Dragon. The Dragon may have already been slain by Mrs. Cummings, but here on this fucking sand-covered atoll, John was going to do the same. I watched his eyes steadily scan the ocean and sky, and I realized that as far as he was concerned, any approaching enemy was the Dragon, and he was going to defeat the roaring beast once and for all.

I glanced to my sides. Dan had paired up with Gary to help load the weapon with John instead of Bill, no doubt to help the young man, who reminded him in many ways of his own brother. John, Dan, and Gary were to my right, while Bill was to my left lining up the sights and preparing the gun for me to fire. The guns were spread out along the coastline of Peale; the nearest section to ours was about five hundred yards away. All six coastal artillery guns were armed and occupied, ready for the impending attack. We hadn't been waiting very long—not even a full hour—when we heard the propellers of planes cutting through the air. John and I snapped our necks upward at the sound and observed thirty-six bombers in three V-shaped formations heading for our little island. There was a high-pitched screech as bombs began to fall through the air and penetrate Wake Island. John and I waited for our only officer to give our orders, and we all crouched beside our guns in an attempt to both protect ourselves from the rain of bombs and machine-gun fire that was pouring down upon us, and continue to hold our station.

We heard some large explosions, and I turned my head toward Dan, where he was protectively shielding Gary. John bravely poked his head over the gun and looked toward the airstrip, where the explosions were coming from, and shouted over the explosions and gunfire. "They hit some of the planes! I can't make out how many we have left, but hopefully we'll be able to get some off the ground before they're all destroyed!"

I nodded and held my ground beside him. Bombs and gun fire continued to rain down upon us. We crouched farther into the gun pit in an attempt to shield ourselves from debris.

"We need to dig a foxhole for cover!" Dan shouted at us. Still crouched, we began to scoop out handfuls of dirt and sand to make a deeper hole for us to hide in than the gun pit. I picked my head up briefly and dared to look over the top of the pit and the destruction going on around us. The airstrip was in flames and the bombs kept falling. I ducked back down and continued to dig. All we could do was try to survive the attack so that when our time came we could fire back. I heard engines starting and looked up to see four of our Wildcat fighter planes take flight and begin to return fire at the Japanese aircraft.

John turned to me, and I was surprised to see a triumphant grin on his face. "This is it, Ben!" he shouted excitedly. Together we all loaded our weapon and waited for orders to fire. No ships had been spotted along the coastline yet, but we knew it wouldn't be long before there was. The other battalions across the atoll were doing their best to take down the enemy planes and all we could do was prepare for the time when our guns would be useful. I saw it in John's eyes just before I turned from him and worked on dialing in the shot: this was the epic battle he'd dreamed of since we were kids. Bill and I set the angle of the gun and waited for the order. Today was the day that, for John, we weren't just Marines—we were knights.

"Ships spotted!" The officer shouted, passing along the coordinates we needed to set our guns to. We waited for the order, watching the ships approach the islands.

"Fire!" the officer screamed somewhere beside us. I fired the coastal artillery gun, and we started the process over. That day, John was Lancelot and I was his trusty squire. No longer were we marching into battle; battle had found us, and we met it head-on with swords swinging.

December 11, 1941

The battle raged on. Some civilian workers that were helping to build the airstrip had been able to bring us some water and a little bit of food over the past couple of days, but there hadn't been much time to stop and rest. With all the adrenaline, I don't think we could have rested anyway. It turned out that in the first bombing raid, the Japanese took out eight of our twelve planes, leaving only four able to fly. Every now and then I would turn my head skyward and watch as Jim's section attacked the enemy aircraft that were still in the air. He may have been an ass-twat and a downright unpleasant person, but damn, that kid could fly. I was very thankful then that he was on our side. I looked over at John and noticed his shoulders were starting to slump, but he kept pushing on, his hunger and fatigue never slowing him down. I did what I could to remain at his pace, knowing that he was right in maintaining it.

"The enemy is trying to land! Men, hold your positions!" The officer shouted over the blasts. I bent down and tried to ready my coastal artillery gun by starlight. I had lost all track of hours, but my weary body told me that it was sometime in the early morning. The stars twinkled above, and I could feel the sparkling eyes of my heroes watching me as John and I followed in their footsteps and worked to defend life and liberty.

"Fuck!" I heard the once timid voice of Sweet Gary shout.

I looked up, and both John and I paused in our actions to make out the force that was headed toward us. In the darkness it was nearly impossible to make out anything but dark shapes in the distance, but due to the constant fire that was raining in the sky, it illuminated the shapes from time to time. "Is that …" I said, too surprised to move. I saw John nod out of the corner of my eye. He was just as stiff as I was, but unlike me, his voice didn't quaver when he spoke.

"Looks like destroyers coming our way," he stated matter-of-factly.

I nodded and proceeded to prepare my weapon. It baffled me how John could remain so calm. The more I thought about it, though, that's what made John such an excellent fighter. The whole reason he'd been able to bail me out my entire life is because he had that uncanny ability to remain calm. I, on the other hand, always got swept up in the action, and I would twist and turn myself around in it until up was down and right was left, and my lips kept firing idiocies like armor-penetrating bullets that got my ass kicked. The only reason things were different now was that I had to wait to fire my weapon. If it were a free-for-all, you can bet your ass I'd fire at anything moving out there until all my rounds were gone. Luckily, that was not the case.

"Lieutenant, they're gettin' closer!" Bill said to the officer in charge as we all watched the now visible six destroyers, three light cruisers, and two troop carriers make their way toward our beach.

"Not yet! Hold your fire! Devereux wants them closer." the officer said.

I let out a deep, shaky breath and felt my hands start to sweat. John looked over at me, and I saw that despite the exhaustion, his eyes were still clear and bright and steady. I turned back to the darkened figures of the destroyers coming our way and felt fear tighten around my heart and swell in my chest until I could hardly breathe.

"John!" I shouted over the sounds of the guns in the air. John turned back to me from watching the enemy ships approach our tiny beach where our six guns stood between them and the land. I licked my lips and grabbed his hand, roughly shoving it on the gun and pushing myself from behind it. John followed my lead and switched places with me, leaving my unsteady hands to refill the weapon instead of continuing to fire it. John nodded at me; I let out an unsteady breath and nodded my thanks in return. I had been firing the gun for the past day, and after seeing the destruction that was headed our way, I could no longer suppress my overwhelming fear. I looked back toward the beach and was glad I had switched with level-headed John. The destroyers couldn't have been more than four thousand yards away.

"Open fire!" Major Devereux had sent the command and the officer shouted it down to us, giving us the final order to shoot the approaching enemy ships. I reloaded after our first shot and watched as John, a burning fire of excitement and honor in his eyes, fired the gun with accuracy. Dan, Gary, and I were already reloading the gun so that Bill and John could line it up and fire again when we saw the first round explode and hit one of the destroyer's magazines. I heard a loud shout come from Bill as he fired. Time slowed; we watched the enemy destroyer explode with a hot blast of air sent in all directions; it sank in two minutes. It was too dark to tell if any of the men on board made it out alive, but there was a lack of splashing to indicate soldiers swimming toward land. The soldiers manning Battery L all broke into a delightful cheer and continued to fire, damaging a cruiser and three other destroyers. The sky soon started to lighten, and we heard the hum of the Wildcats in the air as they flew over us and toward the remaining destroyers. Somewhere beside me, Dan whooped enthusiastically as the Wildcats dropped a bomb on the stern of a destroyer and sank it before our eyes.

I watched John's eyes light up and knew that he had just accomplished an amazing feat. Not only had he contributed in sinking a destroyer and defending our little sandbar and fighting off the Japanese so that America could fight them for one more day, but he had also defeated that Dragon of his past. With one explosion, the demons of his soul were slaughtered and destroyed. With each thud of the artillery guns as they fired, he killed the dragon that lurked within him.

"They're retreating!" Gary shouted, pointing at the remaining destroyers and light cruisers as they pulled back from their first landing attempt. I let out a triumphant laugh and clapped John enthusiastically on the back. He looked up at me then, that energy of his wrapping around me and pulling me in. His eyes were no longer shielded, and they reflected all the happiness and freedom he had never allowed himself to express before. His internal shackles had been broken, and now he was finally worthy enough in his own eyes.

December 23, 1941

Twelve days after John helped sink the destroyer, the battle continued to rage. Commander Cunningham had sent a request for supplies necessary for us to continue fighting the enemy off, but he said that the ships with our reinforcements were told to turn around and head to Pearl Harbor for fear that they would be attacked before they reached us. It'd been fourteen days since the enemy attacked us that morning of December 8, and we all knew that without supplies our chances of winning this thing were now pretty much nonexistent.

It was well into the night and we were given a brief reprieve from the battle while both sides took time to regroup and strategize the next approach. I was leaning against the gun, my head propped up on the base for support against exhaustion. Bill was snoring to my right where he had propped himself up against the other side of the gun mirroring my position. I looked over at John to my left where he lay curled up in a ball in the pit; he had dozed off. We'd been lucky if we could catch an hour of sleep here or there, but with the adrenaline constantly coursing through us, it didn't make much of a difference whether we slept or not. We'd alternated positions a few times over the days since the first landing attempt, when we sank two destroyers.

I'd spent some time with Gary reloading the gun, trying to cheer him up by cracking some inappropriate jokes. He'd give a polite smile for me, but I knew there was nothing I could say or do that would make the kid forget about mortality and how short life can really be. John tried talking to him about books and philosophical thoughts on life and what comes after. That seemed to both depress Sweet Gary more as well as relax him about the whole thing. And Bill—well, we should never have let him talk to Sweet Gary. All he said was, "Well, come on, we all knew that war meant we were probably gonna die. This is what ya signed up for, kid! Just be happy knowin' that you're goin' down for them pretty ladies ya got at home!" Then he slapped him roughly on the shoulder, turned around, and fired his rifle at an enemy plane flying overhead. It wasn't long after that that Dan kicked Bill out of the bottom of the pit and sent him back to the top where he was originally setting the coordinates and lining up the shot with me and away from Sweet Gary.

I turned my head away from the dozing John and looked to the foxhole we had dug out, where Dan and Gary were taking the time to rest as well. Dan opened his eyes and looked over at me, a small smile on his face. He turned his head toward the stars, which were bright and twinkling down at us from the midnight sky. "John told me that ya know quite a bit about them stars, Ben," he said. His voice was scratchy from yelling over the sounds of bombs and gunfire, and from a lack of water. A civilian was able to come by during these breaks and give us some supplies, but without the restock from the mainland, the ration sizes of food, water, and even ammunition kept getting smaller.

I smiled at Dan and turned toward my heroes in the sky. Perseus twinkled down at me, and I nodded. "I sure do. John was always into that snooty philosophy and literature crap. I preferred to look at the world around me," I said.

Dan grunted again as he resituated himself to get more comfortable and moved Gary so that he was sleeping soundly on Dan's shoulder. "Why's that?" he asked interestedly.

I smiled wider and let out a hoarse chuckle. "Oh, come on, Dan. Philosophy? Literature? It's hard enough for me to understand the fuckin' people around me that I care about; why would I ever be interested in strugglin' to figure out what all the intellectual types around the world are thinkin' about? People baffle me, which is why I mostly don't give a shit. But nature, ah, now there's somethin' that makes sense."

Dan chuckled, and he coughed because of the dryness of his throat when he did. "How does it make more sense to ya than people?" he asked.

I shrugged, my eyes still trained heavenward. "Because nature does things with purpose. It rains to water the plants and animals. Trees grow to get more sunlight so that they can produce more oxygen through photosynthesis; trees drop leaves in the winter so branches don't break from the weight of ice and snow. It's all necessary for the earth to keep goin'."

"And the stars?" he asked while looking at the bright, faraway beacons.

"The stars ... well, those I'm still trying to figure out. They could be the light from millions of other worlds that vanished eons ago, or simply a way for gods of past and present to immortalize the heroes of our world. See there ... that's Perseus. He defeated the sea monster sent by Poseidon to devour the princess Andromeda." I traced his noble figure with my finger so Dan could find him in the sky.

"Sounds like ya got a better handle on this philosophy stuff than youse might think," Dan said under his breath. I glared down at him, my eyes squinting to make out his figure in the darkness even though he was only a yard or two away from me. Dan just laughed and said no more about philosophy after that. "So is Perseus your favorite then?" he asked amusedly.

I leaned away from him finally, after feeling that I had sufficiently made my point. I nodded again and traced his gleaming outline in the stars once more. "Yup. Him and Orion," I said. Dan prodded for me to explain further, which left me stumped for a bit. "I'd never really put much thought into why they're my favorites. I guess I like Perseus so much because he took on all these quests and solved them all, slaughtering monsters like Medusa and rescuing dames like Andromeda. I guess in a way he makes me think of John, and it's kinda like lookin' up and seein' my buddy up there. All fables and glory—with an unrealistic sense of honor to boot." I glanced down to make sure that John was still sleeping, and to my relief, I could still see the steady rise and fall of his sturdy chest.

"I guess I can see that. But what about Orion? What'd he do that was so heroic?" Dan asked.

I looked back at the stars and found Orion and his sparkling belt low on the horizon. I shrugged and turned toward Dan. "He didn't really do anything. He was a hunter—the best, in fact. There are several different versions of his life and death. My favorite is that he used to hunt with the goddess Artemis. She loved him very much, and this caused her brother to hate Orion. So one day he tricks Artemis into shooting a far-off mark. She does, and because she was an expert archer, she hit her target and killed it. Well, it turns out that this target was in fact Orion, and Apollo had tricked Artemis into accidently killin' him. She was so devastated that she raised him into the heavens and made him out of stars."

Dan just stared at me for a minute in contemplative silence before turning to Orion's figure on the horizon. "Why on earth is that your favorite? I mean, Perseus I get. He was a hero—chopped heads off, rescued ladies, and the like. But why some unimportant hunter that was accidently killed?"

I chuckled at Dan's confusion and shook my head. "I dunno. I told you I never really thought of it before. I guess that's why I like him so much. He didn't really do anything of great importance, but he meant an awful lot to one person—enough that she wanted to immortalize him forever with other heroes in the sky. That's his honor." I said, a small smile on my lips.

"Bein' put in the stars? Yeah, I guess it don't get more honorable than that. It's sure better than a measly badge, anyway." Dan chuckled drily.

My eyes remained fixed on the constellation above us and I shrugged. "Not just that, but that someone cared that much to put him up there. I guess it just proves everyone's important to someone, even if they're not important to everyone else." I said, glancing down at Dan before I turned away from him. He chuckled once more, and I heard him mutter quietly to himself, saying something like "fuckin' philosopher," but I couldn't be too sure. I leaned forward and stretched my back out, feeling the vertebrae in my spine pop and crack. I stretched my arms above my head and turned to look at John. His eyes were closed, but his chest was struggling to resume the steady breathing it had been doing moments ago. I ignored it and lay back down.

◆ ◆ ◆

I must've dozed off for an hour or two, because the next thing I felt was John shaking my shoulder and pushing me up until I was sitting upright.

"What's goin' on?" I asked, wiping the sleep out of my eyes and slapping reason and alertness back into me with a few light, open-palm smacks to my cheeks. John and Bill continued to fuss about the coastal artillery gun to get it ready while he filled me in.

"Seems like they're trying to land again! They're bringing more destroyers and cruisers. We don't have enough ammunition to hold them off. Major Devereux says to ready ourselves for combat." John's voice was steady and authoritative as he continued to prep himself for the coming onslaught. I scrambled to my knees and began to assemble and load my operable rifle. Captain Michaels would be so proud, I thought. I shook the sand out of the magazine before loading it and made sure I had my refill cartridges in my pockets. Fucking sand! Always where it's not supposed to be.

"Fire!" The Lieutenant shouted, commanding us to fire what remaining ammunition we had at the approaching army. We got a few shots in, but none were able to sink any of the destroyers or cruisers. "Prepare for combat!" The officer shouted. My heart was pounding so hard I felt like it would leap out of my chest, grab a rifle, and start shooting. The blood was pounding so loudly in my ears that I barely heard Bill's excited whoop from somewhere to my side. I looked at John to see if there was fear in his eyes like I knew my own were swimming in. Instead he just turned to me with the biggest fucking grin on his face and his eyes twinkling joyfully.

"This is it, Ben! This is our battle, our quest! Let's ride into like the knights we are!" he shouted, his voice dripping with excitement that only succeeded in terrifying me more. I heard a screeching sound as a Japanese bomb sailed through the air toward the sand beach of our little atoll. There was a loud bang, and sand and metal flew about as the bomb connected with the earth. I ducked down, Mrs. Cummings's voice echoing in my ear, saying something about protecting John. I felt a warm, heavy weight press upon me as John flung himself over my hunched form. Yeah, right, I thought. Me protect him? Sure. My ears rang with the echo of the bomb's explosion.

I felt John lift himself off of me, and I sat up, my eyes squinting in the clouded air to see where the bomb had hit. The air settled enough for me to make out the hunched figures of the section that was closest to us on our right. Bill leapt out of the gun pit and rushed toward one of the privates that had been tossed out of the pit by the explosion. The private was on his stomach and groaning, his hands flailing in a weak and shocked attempt to roll himself over; his legs had been blown almost completely off.

Bill was trying to pull him away from the pit where the other men of his section were resting in pieces so he could remove the shrapnel from the private's remaining thighs and back. Bill had been wounded himself because he had been toward the top of our pit when the bomb hit, taking some fragments of the bomb in his shoulders. John rushed over to the two of them and began helping Bill tear tourniquets out of his massive shirt.

"It ain't so bad, man; just hang on!" Bill shouted reassuringly to the private. John lifted the man's legs so that Bill could tie the makeshift tourniquets around the bloody stumps. I slowly rose out of my gun pit and made my way to the dying man. I ignored John and Bill and knelt down at the private's face, gently lifting it up and brushing the sand off of his cheeks.

The man's wide and panicked eyes met mine, and I inhaled sharply at the terror and pain that filled them. I hardly knew this man; hell, I didn't even remember his name, but I'd seen him around during training and preparation. I watched the warmth in his eyes drain out, replaced with the flooding coldness of death. I wished I had known him better. He took one shuddering breath, his flailing hand coming to rest upon my shoulder, and his eyes no longer stared into mine but detached to stare at something in a far-off place. His hand fell lifelessly from my shoulder and dropped down to the sticky, blood-drenched sand. I lifted my head up and watched as Bill and John hurriedly tried to stop the still bleeding wounds, completely unaware that the man had died.

"Stop," I said. John and Bill didn't seem to hear me and kept working. I reached out and put my hands on their bloody, heroic ones, forcing them to look up from what they were doing and into my eyes. Bill looked at me with confusion all over his face, and John looked at me with a mixture of annoyance and scorn. I shook my head slowly and brought their attention to the lifeless features of the man lying in my lap. John lowered the man's leg gently and nodded in sadness. Bill simply let the man's leg fall with an ungraceful thump and ran his bloody fingers through his dark hair. John and I stepped back as Bill opened up and bellowed into the early morning air.

"Here they come!" Dan shouted across the line. We all turned away from the dead private and watched as hundreds of enemy soldiers landed on our beach. Bill growled like a primal beast and grabbed his rifle.

"Fuckin' brutes!" he shouted furiously before charging toward them. Gunfire began suddenly, and the very sound felt like needles of terror being hammered into my very soul, each one reiterating that this was war and humans are mortal—that I was mortal.

John rushed back to our pit and grabbed our rifles. I walked over to him and took mine from his steady hands when he offered it to me. The excitement had returned to his eyes; they were a little tamer now but had much more stubborn abandon behind them.

"Let's go!" he shouted. He started to dash into the fray, but I plunged my arm out and grabbed his shoulder, forcing him to halt his aggressive charge. He spun and looked at me expectantly. I looked over my shoulder at the dead private and then turned to look into the battle, where Bill was fighting furiously. I licked my lips and gripped my rifle and his shoulder tightly.

"We're not knights, John! You know that, right? This isn't just another one of your books, and the hero doesn't always win! You know that, don't you?" I shouted over the gunfire and falling bombs.

I heard a bellow in the fighting on the beach, and we both turned to see an enemy soldier thrust a knife into Bill's chest and twist it agonizingly. Bill dropped to his knees in pain, and the soldier pulled his knife from Bill's chest and shoved it into the side of Bill's skull. Bill's agonized yell quickly cut off, and he dropped lifeless onto the sand. John turned back to me then, his eyes burning with a fire that I thought he had killed when we sank the destroyers.

"Doesn't matter, Ben! We are knights because we know it in our hearts! Now stop acting like a fucking girl, and let's show them just how noble we can be!" With that, he charged toward the advancing soldiers. I began to hyperventilate, watching John's figure get smaller before it was consumed by the battle, and seeing Bill's lifeless form simply ignored as soldiers fought around him as though he had never existed in the first place.

Unable to watch anymore because the fear was coiling and tightening around my chest so hard it was painful to breathe, I looked over to my side, where Dan was giving Gary the ultimate pep talk. Gary's face was like stone, and even though his hands shook a little with fear, his jaw was set and his gaze was hardened for battle. Dan smiled at him and comfortingly patted his shoulder one last time. Dan turned from Gary and looked over at me, and with one nod in my direction, he was off into the fray.

I took a deep breath, knowing that John needed me beside him rather than being a coward in the dark, so with Gary following my steps, we followed John and Dan into the fight. I soon lost sight of Dan and Sweet Gary, but I kept pushing through and shooting at the enemy soldiers in my path until I came upon John.

John spun around, his rifle poised and ready to fire, but he stopped when he saw it was me. He smiled at me, his face filled with pride and boyish glee that his friend had made it to his side. For the most part the enemy soldiers had spread out, and the battle was raging across the atoll and in the sky, where our four Wildcats no longer flew, the last having been shot down two days earlier.

"How'd you find me?" John asked, reloading his rifle with his last clip. I laughed a little at that, my eyes scanning the beach for any enemy soldiers headed our way.

"Come on, what kind of knight would you be without your fuckin' squire?" I said, waiting for him to rearm himself.

John chortled and finished reloading. "Where would I be," he said to himself.

Together we checked the beach and killed any enemies we came across, but there weren't many left at the shoreline from the first wave of men that had landed on the beach. There were more ships on the horizon coming closer, but there was nothing we could do about it.

"Most of the fighting is moving inland!" John shouted over the rain of bullets in the air. I nodded and followed him back up the beach and closer to Battery L headquarters. As we got closer to headquarters, we could just barely make out the shapes of two marines as they battled several enemy soldiers on the outskirts of our camp. There were only two lanterns in this area, and one inoperable truck a hundred yards away to the right of the camp as we approached. The lack of light made it difficult to make out what was going on, but it was obvious that they weren't using their weapons; instead, their rifles had been cast aside and lay uselessly in the sand.

They were fighting in hand-to-hand combat, and it was apparent that the two Marines were outnumbered and overpowered. One of the Marines was small and frail looking, while the other was larger and very muscular and was expertly defending himself and the smaller man from the enemies. The larger man managed to drop a few of the enemy soldiers, evening the numbers to two-on-two. As we got closer, the lanterns at HQ swayed in the warm, tropical breeze and illuminated a swatch of bright-red hair.

"It's Gary and Dan!" I shouted at John, and we both picked up our pace and ran toward our friends. We were about a hundred feet away when one of the enemy soldiers shoved Gary roughly away from him and pulled out a small pistol from his boot. Gary flopped harshly onto the ground from the force of the enemy's shove. He rolled onto his back, prepared to continue fighting, but the enemy thrust his pistol into Gary's face.

John and I ran faster, pushing our exhausted limbs to keep going, ignoring the burning in our muscles. When we got closer, we both brought up our rifles and prepared to take aim at the man pointing his pistol in Gary's face, but before we could fire, we heard a booming howl as Dan pushed the man he was fighting aside and threw himself on Gary. Dan's loud howl seemed to throw the gunman off for a second, just long enough for Dan to push Gary aside and for us to take our aim. It seemed that it was almost simultaneous; as John and I pulled our triggers, so did Gary's opponent.

There were several loud cracks as bullets were released from their chambers and soared into their intended victims. The enemy gunman doubled over and was thrown off his feet as John's and my bullets sunk into the flesh of his proud chest, and he fell dead. The remaining soldier that had been fighting Dan tried to stand up and regain his shaky footing to attack us, but John whipped around and shot him. John dropped his rifle and we both rushed to our fallen comrades and tried to assess the situation.

"Oh God," I said sadly as I looked into the face of my dead friend. I knelt down beside Dan, setting my rifle carefully beside me. I brushed the hair back from his forehead, and boy there was a lot of it, and tried to wipe the dripping blood from his lifeless eyes. The gunshot to the side of his head oozed, and pieces of his scalp and hair lay fragmented in the surrounding sand. I felt my eyes sting with the pinpricks of tears that dripped silently from my eyes. I heard a soft cough and quiet weeping from behind me. I looked over my shoulder and watched John comfort a sobbing Sweet Gary.

"Why would he do that?" Gary asked, his green eyes swimming with guilt and pain. I looked down at Dan's paling face and stood up, moving away from him and toward Gary. John remained silent and continued to rub Gary's back gently. I squatted in front of Gary so I could be at his eye level. Gary just stared into the vacant brown eyes, which were nearly obscured by thick eyebrows and congealing blood.

"Because you reminded him of his brother," I whispered to Gary. "And he wasn't about to lose another little brother." Gary's eyes moved away from Dan's body and came to rest on my face. None of us said anything more, and Gary quickly stopped sobbing and wiped away his tears. Gary carefully pushed himself up until he stood over the kneeling John and my crouching figure.

John and I slowly got up, watching Gary's motions very carefully as we did. He didn't say anything more; he didn't even look at Dan's body again. All he did was bend down and grab the pistol lying off to the side of the fallen gunman. He looked at it a moment, turning it over in his hands before glancing up at the two of us one last time and running off into the sound of combat.

"Shit!" John said, and he ran toward his rifle, which he had dropped in the sand once we shot the enemy soldiers. I began to follow suit and bent down to pick up my own that was lying by my feet resting beside Dan's body, when I heard a screech pierce the air, and I paused. I looked up and saw a bomb plummeting toward us.

"John!" I yelled. John spun around at the sound of his name, his rifle lying at his feet, two hundred feet away from where I was standing. I was about five hundred feet from the truck and John was closer to seven hundred feet from it. It was only seconds later that the bomb struck the inoperable truck and exploded in metal fragments and burning flames. I was thrown off balance and pushed into the sand by the force of the explosion behind me.

My head was pounding and my ears were ringing. I could barely hear John shouting my name, and I tried to reply, but it only came out as an incomprehensible groan. John was lying on his side somewhere to the right of me. There was a blinding pain in my side. Fuck, it hurt. I wasn't entirely sure where I had been hit; my entire torso felt as if it were on fire. I tried to move my legs and was surprised to find I could. Well, that's a good sign. The way the heat was filling my stomach and the pain was slicing through me, I had been afraid that my legs were lying some three yards off. At least I was in one piece. Kind of.

John coughed, and I heard him throw up and groan. Asshole, when did he get something in him to throw up? I struggled to roll over, but I was determined to make sure he was okay. I tried to lift my head, but when I did, a blinding pain shot down my spine, and I bit down on my lip to keep from whimpering like a punk. I heard some scuffling and some deep groans as John attempted to push himself up. I couldn't see him, but I knew he was trying to crawl toward me.

I opened my eyes a little bit, hardly enough to make out anything more than blurry colors, let alone shapes. I could smell the sand that my cheek was pressed so firmly into. Fucking sand. I curled my hand into the fucking sand, and it felt more than just granular; it was warm and surprisingly sticky. I didn't have to look at the blurred colors to know it was blood. That's not good. I felt John slide up next to me, his shuffling drowned out by the nearby shouting and screaming as bombs sank through the air and exploded on the earth. I felt his warm hands on my arm; they were sticky too. He slowly turned me onto my back, and I gave it my all to open up my lazy eyes. I felt another blinding pain when I did so, and I found there were white spots in my vision. I stared up at John as he slowly transitioned from colored blurs to geometric shapes until he was finally himself.

John had sand sticking to the left side of his face, where there was a nice stream of blood oozing out of a gash on the top of his head. His eyes looked into mine, and I could see all the notes from training about medical procedures flashing in those blue eyes. His eyes looked over my face and then slowly, calculatingly, down my body. He didn't say anything, and he didn't move or panic or start screaming in agony. Nah, that wasn't John. He just closed his eyes and lowered his head—only the slightest bit, but I saw it.

"I can … move my … feet; look," I said proudly. Fuck, my throat hurt. It was dry, and once again I was slightly envious that John had been able to throw something up. I managed to flip my right foot over and jerk it a little in attempt to cheer him up. I saw a small smile tug at the corner of his left cheek. Ah, there it is. I was hoping I'd see that "you're an idiot" smirk.

John slowly turned his head back to me, and I saw a piece of shrapnel sticking out of his shoulder. I tried to push myself up, but that heat in my stomach shot out through my entire body, making me feel as though I were on fire. John tried to stop me; I could see the panic in his eyes. Fuck it.

I pushed myself onto my forearms and looked at his injuries. He had the shrapnel in his right shoulder; what it came from I had no idea, perhaps the truck that exploded or the airstrip, or the bomb itself. The gash on his head was starting to clot, but blood drenched his collar. I sat up a little further, pushing against that damnable heat. It also looked like something had cut his side, perhaps more flying shrapnel. I thought that maybe he was feeling the same heat that I was.

"You probably shouldn't move, Ben," John said softly, with a hint of that scolding tone his mom would use when we dragged dirt into the house, or when I came too soon.

I swallowed in attempt to make my throat less dry. "Nah, I'd rather … not lie here like … a little bitch." I smiled at him, and he chuckled a little. His chuckle had pain in it, and I could see him wince and fold into himself a little. He nodded. My eyes were still blurry, and it took effort to try to focus on anything, but because of the difficulty to focus, it was easy to spot things that moved unexpectedly.

I noticed an enemy soldier approaching us from the direction of the beach, where we had come from, his bayonet raised and ready to pierce John in the back. I reached beneath me and grabbed my rifle. I dropped to the sand without the support of both arms, wincing as my back connected with the ground and shot a blinding heat from my abdomen through my spine down to the tips of my fingers and toes. My grip was weak, but I still managed to bring it up and aim it over John's wounded shoulder.

The enemy soldier halted briefly before snarling and letting out a battle cry as he ran toward John and me. John tensed, increasing the flow of blood dripping from his wound, and looked over his other shoulder at the sound. I squeezed the trigger with all the strength I had left in my hands, making John wince at the loud report of my rifle beside his left ear. The soldier dropped in his tracks, his bayonet impaling the ground a few feet away from us, and he lay there facedown, the life draining out of him through the hole my bullet had made in his throat.

John turned back to me with a huge smile on his otherwise saddened and pained face. "You didn't miss that time," he said with a chuckle.

I smiled proudly up at him and dropped my rifle. That should be enough to make Mrs. Cummings happy. "See ... where would you be without me?" I said comically.

John chuckled softly, pathetically, sadly. "Yeah, where would I be," he whispered back to me. He smiled sadly at me and looked me up and down once more. "Can you hold yourself up?" he asked, already knowing the answer to the question.

I didn't have to answer; I just blinked at him and he was already shuffling himself into position behind me. When I felt his back rest against my head, I began pushing myself up. It felt as if John's dragon had taken a bite out of my stomach and filled it with flames. I felt his back rise and fall with each shuddering breath that he took as I slowly inched myself up. When we were back-to-back, I let my head sink down onto his shoulder and just listened.

His breathing was more ragged than I had originally thought, and I could feel the sharp intakes of his breathing every now and then. Though he tried to muffle them with coughs, I could hear the whimpers of pain he let out. The shouting was moving farther away from us, and the sky was no longer being lit up by bombs like fireworks ... like the fucking Fourth of July. I tilted my head up and felt the stickiness of John's blood in my hair as I did so. The stars were still brightly visible even though dawn was approaching. I smiled to myself and let out a shaky breath. I did so love to stare at the stars, even if they were tainted with the warm glow of fire and the harsh pink of sunrise.

"Ben, you're going to pull through this," I heard John say to himself. I just smiled as I stared at the stars and let my head drop to one side. "We are going to get through ... this." He took a deep breath that filled his frame and slowly let it out. I felt him tense as the air escaped his lips in a low whistle. "We're knights, Ben."

I smiled and let my head tilt against his in agreement. I felt him chuckle a little; it was strained, but it still shook his body against my spine. The movement sent a shock through my body, but the heat quickly devoured it. The heat wasn't as bad anymore—it almost felt comfortable.

"Nah, John ... I'm no knight ... that was always ... you." I hated that my throat was still so dry. I felt his body crumple a little as he folded into himself again. I waited as he took a few breaths and then pushed himself back up.

"You've done everything with me, Ben. You're just as gallant and brave. We're knightly together," he declared.

I tilted my head back toward the stars and watched as they twinkled, untouched by flaws, failures, and pain. My chuckle was raspy and short, but it was the best I could do. "Nowhere close," I said. I smiled and felt him shake against my spine. I wondered if he was getting cold. "I'm just your squire, John. The guy that tags along, making sure you have your sword." At least my throat wasn't hurting as much. I licked my lips and turned my ear to his neck. I listened as his blood pumped through his veins; it was a slow, soothing sound.

"You're better than a measly squire, Ben," he whispered, and I felt the muscles in his neck tense by my ear. I could feel that he was holding back a sob as he shifted his bleeding side wound. I stared at my heroes in the sky as they slowly started to fade in the light of day. Orion was disappearing first because he was the lowest on the horizon, the sunlight devouring him.

"Hey, what was it that Dan told you back before this all began?" I asked, the incident becoming quite clear in my mind. My eyes drifted away from the brightening sky and found the spot where Dan's corpse still lay. I felt John inhale against me once more and let his breath out with a shiver against my back.

"He told me that I ought to listen to you more. That you have a lot more to say than you let on and that if I just stop being such a pompous ass, I might actually get to know you as well as you know me." I felt him chuckle roughly against my back before hissing in pain.

I smiled at the thought of Dan, knowing that that meddling bastard was probably the only reason John and I were here together right now.

"I gotta admit, Ben. I had no idea you were such a philosopher," John said behind me.

I frowned in confusion, the skin around my temples pulling painfully tight when I did, the dried blood cracking and flaking off my forehead. "I take it you weren't … really sleeping earlier when he and I were talking … about the stars, then," I said in my increasingly raspy voice, the warmth in my torso tightening around my lungs and making it harder to breathe. I felt John shake his head gently against mine. It was just the slightest of jerks from side to side, but I still felt it as his blood-soaked hair tangled with mine.

"Why didn't you ever tell me that stuff about Orion and Perseus?" he asked softly, like a little boy asking why you wouldn't share your chocolate with him at lunch.

I smiled and attempted to shrug but found that the warm heat flared blindingly when I tried. "You never asked … I guess," I replied. My brain was starting to get fuzzy, and it was difficult to remain conscious to converse. I pressed my head into his neck further, smelling blood and sand—fucking sand—and not caring that they were smearing my cheek.

"It's incredible… you know," John said softly, tilting his head toward the sky to look up at the stars I knew so well.

"What's that?' I asked, feeling another shudder go through his body, the force of it shaking my own.

John coughed a little which turned into a dry laugh. "To know someone your whole life, and yet never know them at all. I never knew Orion was your favorite… which one is he?" John asked, tilting his head against mine, searching the stars for an unfamiliar pattern he never looked for before.

My eyes immediately focused on the low-lying constellation, slowly fading in the light of dawn. I smiled a little as the soft glow incinerated his belt and bow. "You can't see him… anymore, the sun's coming up, but… he's low in the southern sky," I told him, trying to lift my hand to point. The heat flared when I tried, so I let my hand drop back down to the sand limply.

John took in another ragged breath. "Oh. You'll have to point him out to me some other time, then." He said. His voice was a little hoarse, but the tone of disappointment was noticeable, even to me. "I need to see this hunter who is so important to you," He said with a sad chuckle. He kept his head tilted to the stars, and I wished I was able to point out all the heroes I knew for him so that he could see them, too.

He let out a sigh and the rise and fall of his chest was so deep, it almost felt like he was breathing with my lungs. It was the first deep breath he was able to take in. "You're right, Ben. It would be a great honor to have someone care so much to put you up there," He said softly, so softly I barely heard him over the slow pounding of blood pumping through his veins beneath my head.

I nodded slightly against his head, unsure whether or not he actually felt my response. "The hero can't die," I said. It came out as a whisper; the heat was beginning to fill my lungs, and it was hard to make sound. I knew he heard me because of the way he tensed against me. John took in a shuddering breath, and as his lungs expanded, his back pushed against me a little. I could feel the strain of his muscles as he tried harder to get another deep breath.

"Yes, he can, but he won't be a hero without his squire—his friend—to tell the tale about him after he's gone," John said. "Who would tell the story then? Who would put it in the stars?" He then started coughing and curled into himself in an attempt to make it stop. I felt him dry heave against my back a couple of times before relaxing. John was panting hard when he leaned his head back against mine. I wondered if perhaps there was more than just flying shrapnel in his side. From the way he was breathing—short and shallow—I thought he must have a broken rib or two.

I let my head drop onto his shoulder and turned it just enough so that I could smell the blood on his collar and glance at the stars out of the corner of my eye. "All right, John," I said with a sigh. "I'll tell your story, but you'd better be around to hear it." I smiled and just listened to his breath as he slowly pressed against me with each inhale.

It was quieter now; the shouting was so far off it was almost inaudible. The sky was darker now, no longer tinged with the glow of war. I wondered how many men had died beneath the stars above. How many men, fighting for something they only half believed in, fighting for something they believed in with their whole heart, fighting to escape, fighting to capture, fighting to live, fighting to lose? How many men had the stars watched bleed out? How many men—cut down by sword, lance, ax, gun, or bomb—had ceased to exist beneath those untouched stars? So many heroes of the past looked on from above, watching as the heroes of the present fell beneath them.

John laughed again, and I felt his head knock gently against mine in a nod. "Someone's got to make sure you tell it right." He forced a chuckle; I could tell because of how he tensed against me and started coughing again. He struggled to stop coughing and to regulate his breathing. I felt his lungs swell against my back in one shuddering breath after another. We sat there in a mutual silence together for a few minutes, listening to each other breathing. He took one deep breath in, and that was the last breath I felt John take. I could no longer feel the sharp rise and fall of his chest against my back. I no longer heard the soft wheeze when he inhaled or the little whimpers he involuntarily let out when he exhaled. His blood was no longer warm and pulsing beneath my cheek. It all had ceased and was gone. I just lay against him, my eyes staring at the stars—white lights twinkling without remorse for having watched another body break and its mortality fizzle out. My twinkling heroes disappeared and were consumed by the cold and blinding light of day.

Melissa Koons

Epilogue
September 1949

It was later in the afternoon on the 23rd of December that the Americans surrendered to the Japanese. It was another few days after that, that the Americans were finally allowed to tend to their wounded and the dead. There were no ceremonies, no individual burials. Everything was quick and timely for the sake of the still breathing; the still living. A few weeks after the Japanese successfully landed and took over Wake Island, they shipped most of the prisoners to a POW camp in Shanghai, China. They were the lucky ones. The remaining Marines and civilians left on the island were murdered by the garrison in 1943 in a brutal retaliation to American Naval strikes on the island.

After the war ended in 1945, the prisoners of war were allowed to return home. The bodies of the civilians and Marines who were murdered by the Japanese Garrison in 1943 were transferred and reburied in Honolulu's National Memorial Cemetery of the Pacific in 1949, including the 47 others that were killed in action during the battle of Wake Island. The National Memorial Cemetery of the Pacific was opened to the public in July 1949, and dedicated on September 2, 1949.

◆◆◆

"It's so green here!" Mrs. Cummings whispered in a shocked but respectful glee. The birds were chirping in the trees at the cemetery, singing happy melodies that made the warm air hum and vibrate. The sun was bright and the sky was blue—so blue that not even pink could stick to it from the sunrise. There was a warm tropical breeze that dried the tears that were trickling down the mourners' cheeks. She turned her beautiful face heavenward and smiled, her blonde curls falling back off her shoulders. She closed her eyes and just felt the warm sun on her upturned face, tears streaming out of the corners of her eyes.

"The sky is so clear here; he'll like that," my mother said as she came to stand beside Mrs. Cummings, my father trailing stoically behind the two women. His face was drawn, and he looked much older than his years. His hair was now streaked with gray around his temples, and his eyes sagged with an exhaustion not caused by anything physical. The group of mourners came to a steady halt before a simple, white, wooden grave marker in the shape of a cross.

Personally, I liked the simplicity of it, but I knew that John would object. It was too simple for a knight. In his mind, we were still knights, even in death—brave men that charged into battle with swords drawn. Maybe in heaven we would be knights too. Perhaps in heaven we'd be true knights with trusty steeds, shiny silver blades, and real dragons to slay. But that sounds like a lot more work than I'd like for an eternal resting place.

"I think he'll just be happy to be out and away from the sand. It was disturbing how much he hated the stuff."

My father turned and looked over at John who had spoken, standing proudly in his marine uniform to his left.

"Really? Ben never seemed to mind it when he was little," my father said, a smile tugging at the corners of his lips as he remembered the days when John and I would build castles out of sand. John chuckled, his lips easily twisting into a grin. He patted my father comfortingly on the back and looked back to my simple grave marker.

"Oh, I reminded him of that myself, but it never stopped him from complaining about it," John answered, his tone light with reflection. "Every day, too. Kept saying it would consume us all. I guess he was right about that. I say it's a good thing he was moved here; he'd probably haunt us forever if he wasn't."

Gary chuckled sweetly beside John. John looked over at the young man, who had grown during the years since his imprisonment in the POW camp; he now filled out his marine uniform nicely. Sweet Gary stood tall and proud, although he was still significantly shorter than John. His shoulders were wider now, and his hair had faded into an auburn color less vibrant than the flaming red it had been eight years ago, when he had run from John and I to avenge the death of his friend. He had a pretty brunette woman holding on to his arm with a soft demeanor and such a delicate properness that it was clear her years at an East Coast boarding school had trained her well. It was obvious that she was attempting to stand straight, squaring her shoulders and elongating the slenderness of her neck as she had been instructed, but the weight of her growing belly caused her back to sway with discomfort.

"That sounds like something Ben would do," Red's gentle voice said. Hell yeah, I would! It had been bad enough having my body buried in the dreadful stuff for the past eight years. If that were my eternal resting place, you could bet that I'd be haunting John until he moved me. Fucking sand.

Red laid a hand gently on John's left shoulder, and John turned to pull the red-haired woman standing behind him into his arms in a comforting embrace. My father chuckled and moved forward to wrap his thick arm around my mother's waist. Red laid her head upon John's strong shoulder and stared at my marker. "I wish I could've gotten to know him better," she said softly, rubbing her hands up and down John's arm.

"Hmm?" John said confusedly. Red looked up and scoffed before walking around him and coming to stand at his other side, where my father had been. He smiled bashfully at her and brought her small hand to his lips.

Gary's wife watched John with a look of confusion on her face. John smiled and pointed to his left ear. "Sorry, you can thank Ben, there, for me being deaf in that ear. He shot an enemy soldier who was coming up behind me, but decided to use my shoulder as a mount."

Red smiled sweetly up at John and ran her hand down the sharp contours of his jaw. "Well, I suppose I can't be too mad at him about it, since he saved your life," Red said, kissing John's cheek. John smiled widely at her and pulled her back to his side. Red sighed and nuzzled into his shoulder peacefully.

"Nah, you could never be mad at Ben for too long," said John. "He was too much of an idiot. It was like being mad at a child that just didn't understand how his behavior was inappropriate. Even our worst fight—a fight that should have destroyed our friendship—only lasted a couple of weeks."

"That reminds me," said Gary. John turned toward Gary, making sure he faced him completely onward so that he would be able to hear Gary's response. "We need to go find Bill and Dan, too. If it wasn't for them, lord knows where we'd all be." Gary smiled sadly, and John nodded solemnly.

The two marines and their loyal wives turned from my grave and began searching for their fallen comrades. It didn't take long before they found the similar white wooden crosses that marked Dan's and Bill's final resting places. Gary lowered his head into his wife's shoulder and tried to hold back the sobs that trembled down his back. John stood straighter and squared his shoulders, tears pooling in his eyes. They stood in respectful silence before the ghosts of their friends, too emotional to say anything and not really knowing quite what to say anyway.

"I owe these men so much. Not just on the battlefield, but off it. If it wasn't for them, if it wasn't for Dan, I probably wouldn't have been with Ben when he died," John said.

Gary nodded and reached out and ran his fingers along the smooth, white span of the cross. "If it wasn't for Dan, I wouldn't be here at all," he said softly. Gary's wife folded into his chest and sobbed softly, one of her hands tracing the panes of his chest beneath his shirt while the other hand gently massaged her belly, which concealed the growing baby inside of her. Gary pulled his hand back form the marker and wrapped his arms around his wife, a peaceful smile coming to his lips.

"Did I tell you, John," Gary said excitedly, pulling John's attention away from the graves in front of him, "we've decided to name the baby Daniel William—or Danielle, if it's a girl." Gary's smile grew and spread across his entire face with a childlike jubilation, just as it used to when Dan and Bill told their crazy stories.

John smiled widely and congratulated the couple enthusiastically. Gary gestured to John and Red with the same excitement and asked, "What about you two? Have you picked out a name yet?" Gary's wife wiped her tears and smiled warmly at John and Red, waiting calmly, but not without excitement equaling that of her young husband.

John and Red both looked down at Red's mostly flat stomach, which barely showed a slight bump. Red looked up at John and shrugged with a smile. "I don't really know. We haven't talked about it much, considering I'm only eight weeks."

John reached down and caressed her tummy over the material of her dress. He shrugged and looked up at Gary with an uncharacteristically large grin. "Perhaps if it's a girl we'll name her Benjamina," he said, winking at Gary. Red winced but quickly tried to hide it behind a grin.

Gary laughed and ignored his wife's confused look. "She'll be a princess; you can count on that! Speaking of Benjamina, we should probably get back to him."

John nodded in agreement and steered Red away from his friends and toward the grave of his squire.

The sun was high above Gary and John as the two of them stood silently before my cross. Mrs. Cummings, my parents, and Gary's and John's wives had retired to a covered area at the memorial to escape the sun, but having spent so many years in the scorching rays without protection, Gary and John were left unbothered.

"I gotta admit," a deep voice said from behind the two Marines, "I never expected it to go the way it did. I always figured that with as much fire as he had in his soul he'd outlive us all." Gary and John turned and watched Jim walk solemnly up to them, his marine uniform pressed and crisp. He came to stand between the two of them, John on his left and Gary on his right, and he stared down at my simple tomb. Jim bent his head respectfully and watched the tropical grass sink and bend beneath the weight of his polished shoes.

John nodded in agreement and continued to stare ahead of him. "Yeah, I always thought the same. But Ben was right; war isn't like a book—it doesn't always go the way you expect, and sometimes … the hero dies."

The three men stood in a contemplative silence for some time before Gary turned to Jim and addressed him directly. "I never thought you'd come here, not given the way you two left things." There was no malice behind his words, no anger or resentment like there had been before the battle.

Jim scoffed and chuckled dryly. "Yeah, well I guess that's why I needed to come. He was a good man, good soldier ... even if he was a pain in the ass." Jim smirked a little, guilt dribbling down his chin. John just stared ahead. He smiled a little and gave a nod to Jim.

None of them said anything more after that. They allowed the silence around them to speak all the apologies they felt in their hearts, before Jim finally turned to go. He paused, facing John, his eyes swimming with guilt. John turned to face him then, for the first time since Jim had arrived, his blue eyes clear and accepting. John smiled at Jim and patted his shoulder. Jim bowed his head, glad for the forgiveness given to him by John. It was almost as good as if I'd forgiven him myself. Which I didn't, but I figured eight years of dealing with the guilt of my death was long enough, so I didn't mind John doing it for me.

Jim nodded and finished turning around. He then squared his shoulders, straightened his spine, and walked away, returning to the world he protected so diligently, the world that John had left behind beneath those stars.

Gary glanced over at John and patted his shoulder. "I'm going to go find the ladies. I'll see you in a bit." He said, giving my grave a final look with a sad smile. He turned and left, leaving John alone with my simple cross and a light breeze.

John stared at the white marker in front of him, a stoic expression on his face. He took in a deep breath that shuddered a little as he released it—a lingering effect from his wounds, his broken rib never had healed quite right. "I hope you know, Ben, if I could, I'd put you in the stars." He whispered. He stood there alone for a moment longer, the silence hanging heavy around him. "You deserve Orion's honor."

He looked down at his hands as tears pricked his eyes before he straightened and composed himself like the knight he was. John didn't stay with me much longer after that. He left to return to Gary and their wives, who were waiting for him under the shade of the memorial.

When he approached, he noticed that everyone in his party had broken off into smaller groups. Gary was standing beside Red and his wife, who had found a bench to rest on. My parents were looking at the memorial; my mother was critiquing the artistry, rambling on and on about the stone and how beautiful the curves were, while my father simply listened. Instead of joining Gary and Red, John headed toward his mother, who was standing in the shade, her back straight, with a small smile on her painted red lips as she reread a familiar yellowed letter. John approached her and simply put his arm around her shoulders. She leaned into the height of her son and continued to read the fading black ink.

"How many times have you read that?" John asked, looking down at the pages that had been folded so many times they were nearly coming apart at the creases.

Mrs. Cummings sighed and continued staring at the letter. "It used to be every night when I first got it; then, as time went on, it became once a week, and now it's faded to only when I really miss him," she whispered, tears leaking out of her eyes and sliding down her rosy cheeks. John hugged her tightly to him and took in a deep breath. "He wrote some very lovely things about you in his last letter, John. I wish you would read it. It was the last letter Ben ever wrote."

John inhaled again and let out a deep, relaxing breath. He smiled into his mother's hair and stroked her back. "I'm okay. I've had my fill of reading Ben's letters. Besides, this one was meant only for you. I don't want to take that away from you by going and reading it."

Mrs. Cummings smiled and closed her eyes peacefully, bringing the letter to her bosom and holding it there. "Thank you for not hating me about the whole situation," she whispered, turning her head into John's chest. John nodded and rested his head against hers.

"Never, Mom," he said, and he kissed her hair. Mrs. Cummings smiled and sighed again in her son's arms.

That day at the memorial, John had that same distant look in his eyes that he had had when he searched that vast ocean during our days on the island. John had successfully slayed the dragon of his father, only for it to be replaced by the despair of my death in the end, and I could tell that he had no intention to try to slay that serpent. He was determined to let it eat a hole in his heart so that it could crawl deep inside and make a cozy den amid the warm, circulating blood.

I suppose every hero has an opponent that he can't defeat, whether it's because he doesn't possess the strength, the weapons, or the will. Now, John's eyes scanned above the horizon, distantly searching the stars like mine had for so many years. I don't need to search for my stars anymore, not from where I rest. And let me tell you, the stars are much brighter from here.

The End

About the Author

Melissa Koons has a passion for history which she incorporates into all her fiction. She writes historical fiction, historical romance, historical fantasy, and short story horror. She also writes non-fiction educational workbooks with the use of her teaching degree and experience. She has a BA in English and Secondary Education from the University of Northern Colorado.

A former middle and high school English teacher, she now devotes her career to being a jack of all trades. She dabbles in publishing, editing, writing, grief coaching, relationship coaching, psychic medium tarot readings, and entrepreneurship. When she's not working on projects or at her beloved 9-5, she's taking care of her cat and two turtles while catching up on the latest comic book franchise or baking show.

Follow Melissa on social media @Write_Koons on Instagram and Facebook.

Keep up to date with the latest releases at
www.writeillusionllc.com

For advice, tarot readings, and coaching services follow Magnificent Musings @Magnificent.Musings.Tarot on Instagram and @MagnificentMusings on Facebook. Visit www.magnificentmusings.com for more details and to book an appointment.

Books by Write Illusion

Fiction
Orion's Honor
Dragon Writers
Undercurrents: What Lies Beneath
Aberration
Mind Rules to End Lost Soul and Body
Shatter Your Image
X Marks the Spot
Hold Your Fire

Non-Fiction
Writing a Critical Essay
Self-Help Blog
Fiction Relationship Analysis Blog

Porcelain Prompts
Fiction
Outlining Your Novel
Creating Characters
Heroes
Villains
Conflict and Resolution
Writing a Series

Available on Amazon, Barnes & Noble, and major retailors online
in both print and eBook formats. Also available on:
www.writeillusion.com
Follow @WriteKoons on Facebook
and @Write_Koons on Instagram

MELISSA KOONS

Mind Rules to End Lost Soul and Body